WAGON TRACKS
ON THE MESA

By Richard C Wright

xulon
PRESS

INTRODUCTION

R ob left the ranch and rode into town, looking for his Pa who didn't return after going in to pay the mortgage. While looking for his father, he makes friends with Betty Sue who he has known for a long time but hasn't really noticed until he meets her when he stops at her father's ranch while searching for his Pa.

SEQUEL BOOKS COMING SOON
By the same author

TRAVELING WEST
A STONE HOUSE FOR THE BRIDE
DUST BOWL CHRSITMAS

ABOUT THE AUTHOR
Richard C. Wright

Not many of this age can boast of living in a log cabin

He was born number three in a large family in Southern Iowa. Because of the Great Depression his family moved into a two room log cabin when he was about two.

In those years much of the farm work was done by horses. He grew up with a love for horses and began riding before he could remember.

He learned a pioneer work ethic and inventive problem-solving in his early years as son of a farmer/rancher in Iowa and later Colorado. While attending Bible College in the heart of St. Louis, Richard met his wife Donna, and began a life-long pursuit of Christian service. His favorite role has always been "pastor", but he has also had a variety of experiences which have given him many stories to tell, Horse trainer, driving instructor, contractor/builder, salesman, estate planner, school administrator, and inventor. Richard's motto is "God never asks you to do anything without giving you the power and ability to do it." You'll see that viewpoint in his stories.

Chapter 1

I had just dozed off when something caused me to come fully awake. Someone was at the front door of the rooming house where I had planned to stay a couple of nights. Without thinking, I dressed rapidly and strapped on my gun, which I seldom wore in town.

Unhooking the screen on the open window, I let myself out onto the lean-to kitchen roof. Standing tight to the building in the shadow, I waited until my eyes adjusted to the dim moonlight. I could see the battered remains of my father's wagon that I had brought in from the canyon today.

Then, out of the corner of my eye, I detected movement in the livery stable across the alley. I look up just as a stranger slipped from the front door of the stable and moved across the alley toward the boarding house.

I'm not sure why my hand moved to my gun, for I had never shot anything but game and rattlesnakes. As the man stepped out of sight, I remembered with a half smile, my Grandpa saying, "Be careful of that gun, son. It'll shoot right where you point it.

One glance showed me the rain barrel almost half full of water. Letting myself over the edge of the roof, I reached my left foot to the rain barrel and giving a shove with my hands, I stepped my right foot to the bolster of pa's wagon and then to the ground out of sight of the window of my room.

I could hear a cruel voice coming from my room demanding, Where is he?" We saw him come in here!" I couldn't quite hear what the landlady was saying, but I could hear the mumble of a scolding voice moving back down the stairway.

Fearing that whoever was looking for me would come to the livery stable; I dodged to the left around the corner of the house, and crouched by a bush that seemed to be growing right out of the foundation.

Breathing a sigh of relief, I mused to myself, "This is out of sight from all directions, unless someone comes down the alley with a light, which is not probable.

Now, I'm not one that usually runs from trouble, and I don't know what made me climb out of that window and stay out of sight. It all happened before I thought about it.

Who were these men anyway? Could they have anything to do with Pa's disappearance?

A lot had happened in the last two days. Two days ago I had come to town looking for my Pa. When he did not return to the ranch after three days from a trip to town to see old man Black and pay this year's payment on the mortgage, I thought something must have gone wrong.

There had been some holdups lately, by Bandit Bluffs near Sand Creek, and ranchers from over our way had begun to hide their billfolds when traveling the main road to town. Old' Bill from a neighboring ranch tells about sitting on his billfold all the way from town, and then just before Sand creek, he had the idea of putting it under the fence staples that were in a pail under the seat.

Pa didn't have much cash on him, for we had sold last summers steers and a few fat cull cows that hadn't calved, to a cattle buyer who brought his own ranch hands and picked up the herd at our ranch. He had given a voucher made out to Pa for cash on demand at the bank in town.

Why were these men after me? Everyone at the café heard and retold the story of my finding and bringing in the broken wagon. Some reported seeing Pa in town and another saw him leave early on the second day. No one saw or heard anything strange, so those that remembered him just thought he had come to buy supplies and by now would be back at the ranch.

After what seemed to be hours and all had been quiet for some time I used the wagon and rain barrel for a ladder and re-entered my room through the window. Not being able to sleep, I sat on the edge of the bed and carefully examined the details of what I had discovered so far.

Two days ago, I had left the ranch early and ridden into town. Trying to retrace Pa's trail, I stopped first at the bank. Mr. Wetmore at the bank said, "Sure your Pa was here and I cashed the voucher, with mostly gold coins, with some silver, for change".

The next stop was Mr. Blacks, but no one answered the door. I thought I heard someone in the house. When no one answered after knocking several times very hard, I moseyed over to the Mercantile where Charley reported that Pa had paid his bill and bought enough supplies to last all winter. The wagon I had found had no supplies or signs of supplies. Now that puzzled me!

It had been a long time since breakfast, so I crossed the street to the café and ordered a hot beef sandwich and a glass of milk.

Living thirty miles from town and only being nineteen years of age, I had not developed many friends in town, so I asked the stranger across the table if he knew Pa. He didn't. So I kept my counsel and finished my lunch.

When I stopped at Mr. Blacks after lunch and asked him when Pa had been by to pay the mortgage, he was nervous at first, then he denied that Pa had been there. He recovered very quickly and told me that I should tell Pa that if he didn't pay the mortgage this week he would send the sheriff out to foreclose, first thing next week.

I thought I knew Pa well enough to know that he would pay the mortgage before he bought supplies. Somehow I felt that something was terribly wrong and Mr. Black knew more than he let on.

My favorite sorrel horse was at the livery stable where I had left him with a double handful of oats and a manger of hay, so he would be rested for the long trip home. On the way to pick him up I had to walk past the saloon. I had heard that it was the place where all the news was passed around, but I knew Pa would not go in the place, so it was of little use to even ask about him there.

At the livery stable I paid the attendant, and saddled up my big sorrel stallion. He was accustomed to having many horses around, but with all the strange horses in the stable he was hard to hold and I was glad to get him on the open road and headed home.

According to the sun it would be dark long before I got to Sand Creek. With all the stories about holdups at Sand Creek lately, I decided to camp early in a wash about five miles before Sand Creek. A little to the south of the main road was a sheltered place out of sight of the road where night travelers would not see my camp. I kicked a hole in the sand, lined it with my canvas ground sheet and poured in half of the water we carried, for my horse to drink.

A man can camp very simply if he has to. I started a small fire with a few dry willow sticks that had fallen to the ground. In cattle country you don't have to go far to find very dry cow chips for a fast hot fire. Breaking off a green branch, I sharpened it and speared six slabs of bacon. While they cooked I cut three slices of bread. When the bacon was done, I wrapped two slabs in a slice of bread and was ready to eat.

Having been raised in a God honoring home, I tossed my hat to the ground and prayed, "Dear Lord, thank you for the grace that gives us the strength to live pleasing in your sight. Help me to find Pa. The food I'm about to eat isn't much, so make it abound as you will for my strength. I ask this in the name of Jesus, my Lord. Amen."

While I was eating, I tried to think where to look for Pa, but I drew a blank, so I checked the tether rope on my horse, rolled out my bed roll and slept, depending on my horse to wake me if we were disturbed.

Just as it began to dawn, I heard my big sorrel make snort and stamped his foot.

Without moving, I opened my eyes to see which way he was looking. He was looking toward the road, with both ears erect. Someone must be traveling mighty early. Without moving the blanket, my hand found my gun and pointed it in the direction the horse was looking. I could see the big sorrel out of the corner of my eye as he watched without a twitch, then he looked my way, lowered his head, nibbled some picked over grass, blew through relaxed lips, a slobbery sound that let me know all is well. He was moving around restlessly so I decided to get up and start the day.

Now when you dry camp on the plains east of the mountains of Colorado, you just don't jump out of the bed roll before light of day without checking for unwanted bed partners, that rattle when they are scared, and bite to defend themselves. So I called the big sorrel. His tether rope let him come with in three feet of me. He lowered his head and made a noise that sounded like a chuckle. I still didn't hear the rattle of the little plague of the desert, so I said, "go ahead and laugh if you want to take chances."

He must have understood, for he shook his head up and down and blew me a slobbery message of affection. It still wasn't light enough to see very far, so I used my boot to kick together the makings I had saved for a morning fire.

I liked to travel light, so the only food was the remains of the pound of bacon and loaf of bread. Making my bacon sandwiches didn't take long; by the time I had finished, it was light enough to saddle up.

Before I rolled up the ground sheet, I watered my horse again. It wasn't much but it would hold him until we got to Sand Creek where we could find water at a ranch about a half mile north of the road.

We turned off toward the ranch and had gone about a quarter of a mile, when I noticed some scuff marks on a bluff too steep for a wagon. I wouldn't have seen them if it hadn't been for the early sun, for three steps forward, they disappeared. Reining around, I looked again and they could only be seen from one spot on the trail. Riding across Sand Creek to get a closer look revealed nothing. Now I wasn't sure if I had seen anything at all. For if they were wagon tracks, the wagon would have had to been pulled up with a rope, for the bluff was too steep for a team.

What I thought I had seen from the road sure looked like about the right distance apart for wagon tracks. The bluff was too steep for a horse, so we moved on looking for a place to ride to the top, then back to where I thought I had seen the marks. After about a half hour, I was about to give up when I saw something just below me in a crevice behind some big rocks about thirty feet down, hidden from all directions, I could see part of the rim of a wagon wheel.

There was absolutely nothing on that bluff to tie my horse to and I knew my horse wouldn't ground tie, even though I had trained him myself. I was never able to get him to ground tie. Pa had said that I was too soft on him and Grandpa said, "You have to be smarter than the horse to teach him anything". Maybe so, he is a mighty smart horse.

I looked around until I found a rock that weighed about fifty pounds, and laid it on the reins, so he wouldn't walk off and leave me while he was looking for something to eat.

Well, it didn't take very long to discover that this was Pa's wagon, but my rope wasn't long enough to snake the broken wagon parts out of the crevice. I had to get the horse closer or get a longer rope. Neither prospect was very likely without going for help.

By now I was getting thirsty and decided to ride over to the Carl Boucher ranch to get a drink and water my horse. I knew Carl, for most of us ranchers who lived farther out on the prairie stopped there for water when Sand Creek dried up in the summer. Carl didn't mind the company for when he was home he usually met us at the well. His windmill was near the lane and he had rigged a tank so travelers could help themselves without opening any gates.

Sure enough, Carl saw me coming and as I watered my horse, he was coming from the barn to meet me.

"Hi there Rob, You run out of work over there at your place, so that all's left is to go to town every week?"

"Hi Carl, have you seen my Pa, lately?"

"Yea, he came by about four days ago for water, said he'd sold some cattle and was on his way to see O.B. Black on the mortgage. What's the matter son, something happened?"

"I'm not sure Carl, Pa hasn't been home and someone has dragged his wagon up on the bluff and dropped it in a crevice."

"I think I know the place, Son, I had a calf fall in up there a few years back. It was quite a job getting him out of there, it took two of us. I had a hired hand at that time."

"Got an extra rope that I could use, Carl? I'd like to get that wagon out of there and look it over."

"Hold on a minute, I have a team hitched up. I was planning to go to town myself, this morning."

"Can you get a team up there?"

"It'll take a bit of doing, but if we go around we can get right to the place."

I saw a movement out of the corner of my eye, over by the house and there stood Betty Sue in a print dress. Wow she was as pretty as a picture. I could feel my ears getting red, as my left hand reached up and touched my hat brim.

"Hello Rob," her voice sounded as relaxed as she looked.

I sure liked the looks of Betty Sue, but somehow when she was around I couldn't find the right things to say, and when I did, it never came out sounding right. So I just smiled and raised my hand part way up again.

Just about then I thought I'd made another of my blunders with Betty Sue.

Carl called to her, "Hey Bets, run tell your mother that I'm going up on the bluff with Rob, and we'll be back shortly for coffee and some of those cookies you were making this morning,"

Tying the sorrel to a post near the tank so he could drink his fill, I walked over to Carl's wagon and climbed in just as he opened the gate, so I picked up the reins and drove the team through. When Carl climbed aboard, he took up the reins and headed in almost the opposite direction from where Pa's wagon was.

Soon we were swinging around the ridge that came out on top of the bluff. This was Carl's range and he knew every foot of it. I could hardly tell we were climbing, but we were soon on the bluff, and when Carl stopped at a place where we could work, he began to unhitch the team, while he instructed me to find my way down to the broken wagon.

Soon we had dragged all of the broken pieces of the wagon up, and I had gathered up all of pa's tools I could find. Pa was handy with tools and always carried some with him, just in case of a break down. Most of the time it was someone else who broke down: for pa kept his wagon in good repair. I also found the ax that he kept sharp, and carried stuck between the front-end gate and the rods that held it in place.

We both looked everything over for something that would help us figure out what had happened. Whoever had done this, had wiped out every trace of evidence; all we had was a broken wagon. They must have thought that we would be a long time in finding it.

I must have stood there in a daze of puzzlement, for Carl began to pull the pins in the tongue and coupling pole. He asked me to find a wrench that would loosen the wheels.

It's surprising how little space a wagon takes up when it is disassembled. Soon all of the pieces were loaded onto Carl's wagon. The back wheels were still in good shape so Carl used a clevis in the coupling pole and hitched them on behind his wagon.

Back at Carl's place the coffee was hot and Betty Sue was just taking a fresh batch of cookies out of the oven, as Mrs. Boucher poured the coffee. We all sat down and Carl told them what we had found.

Mrs. Boucher suggested that we pray right then, that we would find my Pa and that whoever had done such a thing would be found, and punished. Just as I knew he would, Carl bowed his head and began to pray. He talked to God just like He was at the table beside us. You see, Carl and my Pa were leaders in the little country Church that was about half way between our ranches. We didn't have a regular pastor, but we would meet on Sunday morning and one of the men would lead some hymns and another would lead in a Bible study. Sometimes, I think we knew the Bible better than people who had a regular Pastor, because we didn't depend on the Pastor to do our studying for us.

"Son, why don't we leave your wagon loaded right where it is and take it into town. I was going for some supplies anyway. Maybe the sheriff will want to see it and you can have the front wheels repaired."

It was my idea to leave the box and pick it up later, for I could repair the box myself.

I tied the lead rope of my horse to the back of the wagon for I might want to stay in town over night.

So that's how I came to be in town, with someone looking for me after dark when all good people should be sleeping.

Chapter 2

When I went down for breakfast, Widow Miller who owned the boarding house came from the kitchen, carrying a plate of pancakes in one hand and coffee pot in the other. "Who were those men looking for you last night?" The question was asked with a very motherly look of concern.

"I don't know, Ma'am! They might know something about Pa's disappearance."

"Well if you ask me, you had better steer clear of them. They looked like trouble for someone. Say where did you hide? They looked all over for you."

"Yes, Ma'am, I guess I sort of slipped out the window."

"You go ahead and eat your breakfast while it's hot. I hope they never come back. If they do, I'll lock the door and not let the likes of them in my house again."

When Widow Miller went back to the kitchen, I did justice to that stack of pancakes and syrup, and had just leaned back and began the second cup of coffee, when she returned for my plate. True to form she gave me instructions for the day. "You get your-self over to the Sheriff's office first thing, and tell him what happened here last night."

"Yes, Ma'am, I sure will. Ma'am, I'm going to be busy all morning fixing the wagon, so I'll probably eat at the café, and see if I can learn anything about Pa."

Somehow my trip to the sheriff's office didn't add to my confidence in getting much help, but he did promise to investigate. He sure didn't act like he had much time for someone my age. His attitude didn't give me much confidence that he would be much help.

Looking down at some papers on his desk he said, "I want to see that wagon before you move it again; you shouldn't have moved it the first time."

"Sheriff, I need that wagon at home, and if you are going to look it over, you'll have to do it right away, because I'm needed at home, and I will leave town with that wagon as soon as I can get it fixed."

"I may have to hold that wagon for evidence."

"Sorry Sheriff, no can do!" You have Carl Boucher as a witness. Get the blacksmith to look it over, for a witness if you want, for I'm taking it with me."

"See here young man, don't talk to me that way, and don't tell me how to run my business."

"I won't Sheriff, if you don't tell me how to run my ranch."

"Say, young feller, you'd better leave that gun with me, you'll have no use for a gun in this town."

I turned and walked out. This was getting nowhere, and that lazy sheriff didn't seem to have any respect for someone my age. Maybe he didn't know that I had been treated as a man with a full grown brain for several years now, even though I was only nineteen.

Back at the wagon, I looked over the repair job, and decided to do it myself. I was still upset with the sheriff, and wished I had taken the wagon home so I could use our own tools. Now I would have to get help from the blacksmith and that would cost us money that we needed for other things. Pa was handy with tools of all kinds, and working with him all my life didn't leave me far behind, when it came to using tools.

It looked like I would need four wheel spokes for the front wheels. The tongue was broken where the doubletree pin went through it. The spokes and tongue stock I could get from the Wagon Company. The coupling pole we had already shortened beyond the break. It would work until I got home where we had another one.

Looking in the tool box that was left with the wagon I found a hammer and a wheel rim tool that Pa had made by shaping a chisel-like iron to fit over the rim of the wagon wheel, I found some blocks of wood that would work to hold the wheel off the ground so I could knock off the iron rim.

When I got back from the wagon company with the parts I needed, the sheriff and two other men were looking at the wagon. He asked, "Was your Pa carrying much money?"

"I don't think so. He came in to cash a voucher from the sale of calves, and to pay on the ranch mortgage with Mr. Black." I told the sheriff what I had found out, and he left to check on my story.

If you have ever tried to replace spokes in a wagon wheel, then you know how hard it is to get the iron rim back on.

After trying for some time, I finally took the wheels to the blacksmith behind the livery stable and had him heat up the iron rim, then we pounded it on, and cooled it in a tank he had for that purpose.

Before we were through, he offered me a job working for him. It sounded like fun if I were looking for a job, I sure knew I could learn his trade, but there was a problem. He had a daughter about my age, and I figured that he was looking out for a husband for her. I wasn't interested. I could find my own mate when the time came. I didn't think I needed any help.

I knew that his sons didn't want to learn the business, but I think I'd rather run a ranch, anyway.

When I paid the smithy, I noticed some old wagon boards rotted at one end and asked what he wanted for them.

"Take 'em, they're just in the way here, "he offered, with a side swing of his hammer.

"I'll be back for them shortly." I took up a wheel in each hand and began to roll them back to my wagon.

Axle grease? Could I take a chance on making it back to Carl's without any? I was running out of money and I knew Carl would loan me some grease when I got to his place, but that was fifteen miles, on almost dry hubs. As I picked up the boards I looked at the smithy who glanced up from the forge. I motioned toward the grease pail and he nodded, so I picked up the pail and wagon boards that he had given me and returned to the wagon.

When the wheels were on I started on the wagon tongue, marking and drilling the holes with the brace and bit. When I came to the iron that Pa had shaped to hold the neck yoke in place, I noticed that the nuts looked liked they had been off recently. There were different marks that could not have been made by the wagon falling against the rocks.

When I had taken the iron on the end of he tongue off I noticed that there was a hole drilled and plugged.

You know how you feel when someone is watching you? Well, that's the way I felt right then. It may have been just my imagination, but I sure did feel funny. In town there are a lot of people around all the time, but I sensed more than that. I was sure that someone was watching every move I made, but I continued to work just the same.

Pa must have had a reason to drill a hole and hide something here. Just in case someone was watching, I continued with the new tongue, transferring the iron and placing the old tongue on the makeshift boards of the wagon so it could be covered with my saddle and tool box.

After tying everything to the wagon, I make a deal with the livery stable for a horse. I knew the big sorrel would not like it in harness. It always seemed to me that he acted insulted when he had to be harnessed, which never happened very often, because

I always felt sorry for him when we had to harness him, but I just could not afford to rent two horses.

Hitching up my unmatched team of an old horse past retirement, and my very insulted saddle horse, I drove them down the street and tied up in front of the café.

I had just sat down at the big oval table where everyone sat when they didn't want to eat alone, when the sheriff come in. helped himself to coffee and sat down beside me.

"I guess I'll ride along with you out to Boucher's and have a look around."

"Sure!" I would be glad to have the sheriff along, just in case those guys from last night decided to follow.

"Could I talk you into bringing the livery horse back, to save me a trip?"

"I suppose so. What are you going to do about your Pa?"

"Find him."

The sheriff acted like he was going to say something, but instead, cleared his throat, went to the door with an, "I'll be ready when you are."

As we traveled toward Carl's ranch, the sheriff sometimes rode alongside, and then he would ride out a ways as if looking for something. One time when he was alongside, he seemed to be studying me for some time.

Then asked," You and your dad get along all right?"

"Sure, What do you mean by that?

"Oh, nothing, you don't have to get surly."

I don't know why the sheriff should rile me like he did. Only he didn't show much respect for me.

"Pa's about the best father a guy could ask for. He not only loves the Lord, but taught me to walk by faith too. We do everything together. The neighbors say we even think alike."

"Humph! Your Pa works you too hard? I hear tell he works you like a slave."

I didn't bother to answer that remark.

When we started up the Boucher ranch road, I pointed out to the sheriff where I'd seen the wagon tracks.

Mrs. Boucher was on the porch when we rode up.

"Hello! I'll call Carl." She rang the dinner bell and went back into the house.

When the sheriff swung down and began to water his horse, I unhitched the team and pulled the harness off of my horse and fasten it to the harness of the other horse, so when the Sheriff was ready to go back to town, the livery horse would be ready. The big sorrel didn't act insulted any more; his shame left him when the harness come off. When I began to rub him down with the saddle blanket he reached around and nudged me in the ribs with his nose.

By the time I was through with the horses, Carl had come in from somewhere and he and the sheriff were walking toward the porch, talking in low tones.

Mrs. Boucher came out with cups in one hand and coffee pot in the other. "Coffee's ready," she said loud enough for me to hear, so I knew I was to come.

Carl and the sheriff had already found chairs on the porch, and she was filling their cups, when

I walked up and sat on the steps and leaned back against a post. It wasn't until she finished filling my cup and had set the coffee pot down beside me that she said "I'll get you some cookies," then I noticed that Betty Sue wasn't there. It had always been Betty Sue that served the cookies.

When Mrs. Boucher came out with the cookies, she said "Help yourself." Picking up the coffee pot, she refilled my cup. Then speaking low, just for me to hear, "Betty Sue is staying with your mother until you get back, you needn't worry, and she will help with the chores. You can stay here tonight, and go home in the morning.

That sounded good to me, for the sun was low in the western sky and it was still three or four hours to our ranch. After what had happened last night, I didn't really want to travel at night.

After the second cup of coffee, the sheriff stood up handed back his cup with a "Thank you Mrs. Boucher, for the coffee and cookies, we better go have a look see before dark."

Carl's horse was already saddled and tied to the corral fence, so I quickly threw my saddle on my horse and caught up with them half way to the bluff. Now that the sheriff had Carl to talk to, he ignored me altogether. This didn't set well with me for I was used to being treated like an adult at home and by most of the neighbors.

The sheriff spent all his time looking around on the top of the Mesa, trying to find something. All I found was a leather punch and a couple of harness rings that had fallen out of Pa's tool box.

When we got back to the ranch house, the sheriff gathered up the lead rope on the livery horse and mounted up, shook his head and said through a tight jaw, "I just don't know, I guess we will have to bring out a posse and try to find him." Without another word, he rode off. He sure had a long ride after dark ahead of him, but then, that was his job.

"Rob, why don't you help Carl with the chores while I get supper on?" Mrs. Boucher handed me a milk pail. Carl slapped me on the back and said, "Come on son, Old Bossy is waiting to be milked."

Carl stopped by the grain bin, scooped up a small pail of grain and poured it in the trough for the milk cow. Seeing a milk stool hanging on the fence, I took it up in my left hand.

"I guess I can handle this without any instructions," I mumbled to myself.

Old Bossy looked around and went back to eating. Now it doesn't take much mind to milk a cow when you have done it all your life, so I began to think about Pa. Where could he have gone? What happened to him? He was a big man and could take care of himself. No one had heard any shooting. How had they carried away the supplies that were in the wagon? Was he still alive? Somehow I couldn't think of him gone, nor would I believe it until we were sure.

Milking done, I picked up the pail and hung the stool back on the fence and Carl opened the gate so the cow could go back to pasture. We walked up to the back door to find a pail of water and wash pan on a bench that looked like it could be Carl's handy work. Carl motioned toward them, as he took the pail of milk into the house.

He soon came back to wash up himself. "Supper's ready."

We sat down; Mr. Boucher folded his arms and said, "Looks good Ma."

"Thank you, if you'll hand me a bowl, I'll dish up the gravy."

When she had sat down, Carl prayed, "Lord, we thank you for your daily care and provisions, we always need your help, but today more that ever. Can you show us, Lord, how to find Bob McCloud? We ask you to keep him from harm and we leave him in your care. Protect Mrs. McCloud and Betty Sue, and give Rob here the strength of faith to do what needs to be done. Amen,"

"Help yourself to the biscuits, son. You'll need to keep your strength up. It'll be a long day tomorrow."

Now Mrs. Boucher is a good cook, and I hadn't had a full meal since lunch, and I know how to make a cook know you like the cooking, so I filled my plate the second time.

After supper, Carl reached to a stand back of his chair and picked up a Bible. Opening it he read, "Fret not thyself, because of evildoers, neither be thou envious against the worker of inequity. For they shall soon be cut down like the grass and wither like the green herb. Trust in the Lord and do good; so shall thou dwell in the land, and verily thou shall be fed. Delight thyself also in the Lord and he shall give thee the desires of thine heart. Commit thy way unto the

Lord: trust also in Him, and He shall bring it to pass. Psalms 37:1-5."

After he finished, he turned to me and asked, "Rob, would you lead us in prayer?" We all prayed, and when Carl closed with "Amen", he stood up and helped carry the dishes to the sink cabinet.

Carl and I sat on the porch, and after a couple of questions, I told him everything that had happened, except the plug in the broken wagon tongue. That I was sure, contained a clue to the problem, but to keep it safe, I would let it stay until I got home where it could be opened in secret; I thought I knew my father well enough to know what he had hidden there.

Soon it was bedtime, and Mrs., Boucher put me up in Betty Sue's room. Everything about the room reminded me of Betty Sue; it was almost embarrassing to be in her room, even though she wasn't there. Soon weariness from the long day made staying awake impossible.

I woke from a sound sleep with a start. It took a moment to get my bearings; I was brought back to my senses with the smell of frying bacon and boiling coffee.

When I came downstairs, Mrs. Boucher was setting the table for breakfast and Carl was sitting in his big rocker reading his Bible.

After breakfast Carl brought a black mare from the barn that would match the big sorrel in build and speed.

"Not much of a work horse, but on a light wagon she'll move right along."

"It looks like they will make a good team," I observed.

"I'll tie on Bet's saddle and she can ride her home."

"Thank you, Mr. Boucher; I'll see that Betty Sue gets home safely."

What a sorry rig for such a fancy team! Hooked with the black, my horse wanted to show off. Neither horse would be outdone, so a few hours later when we pulled up our driveway, both were lathering around the harness, but both were going strong.

As we rounded the corner in sight of our house, we heard a rifle shot; the team broke into a run without any help from me.

There stood mom with my 45 caliber rifle and Betty Sue with Grandpa's double barrel 12 gauge, pointing right at the middle of two riders.

One of them was saying "Don't get excited ma'am, we just want to look around."

I just drove my team right at the two, and watched them yank their horses out of the way, and then I stopped the team right beside those two riders that looked like they had been on the trail several days with out a shave.

"Watch it Sonny", shouted the tall one, with a slim face and big crooked nose.

He was too busy with his horse to see that I had slipped the reins under one leg so both hands were free and started to raise my hands but instead I dropped my left foot on the left rein and shouted "HAW, Ha, Ha." It didn't sound as much like a laugh as I had hoped, but it did the trick, My big sorrel jerked sideways right into the tall man's horse and when he jumped, my right hand come up with my six gun, "All right, drop those gun belts and back off!

Both rider's right hands moved back toward their guns and I fired a warning shot. His horse must have moved, for the bullet nicked the tall man's ear and knocked his hat back onto his horse's rump and again he fought to control his horse.

Out of the corner of my eye, I saw Betty Sue raise the shot gun to her shoulder, I hoped she wouldn't shoot it. The last time I shot the old gun it almost knocked me off my feet. That gun was dangerous, no matter which end you stood at.

Grandpa had loaned that gun to his brother and it wasn't cleaned properly. The rust pits in the barrel were the size of bird shot.

Those strangers must have gotten the message for they began to rein around and ride away, but I stopped them with, "Hey fellow's you forgot something!"

Now Grandpa had taught me to point shoot, so when the leader reined up as if he would ride away again, I put a shot right between his horse's ears, close enough to burn him. He started bucking like a good feller and put his rider on the ground right on his back pockets.

Stepping off the wagon on the side next to Betty Sue, I handed her the reins of my team and took the old shot gun from her, to make sure she wouldn't shoot it.

"You can drop those guns; you won't need them any more.

Ma had moved up her rifle to point right at the other rider's head. He raised his right hand and was unbuckling his gun belt with the other hand.

I laid the shotgun on the wagon; walked over to the rider getting up from the ground and backed him away from his gun that had fallen out of the holster when his horse was bucking.

I picked up the gun and pointing both guns at his stomach, I ordered, "Take off you boots."

"No!"

"Take off you boots!" and I pointed the left gun at his stomach and right one at his boots.

"You can't do this" he whined, so I shot at his feet, just missing his toes.

He hopped on one foot and took off his boots.

I never took my eyes off him, while I asked Betty Sue to catch his horse.

When she brought up his nervous horse, I handed her his gun and reached over with my left hand and loosened the cinch, dropping the saddle to the ground.

"What ya doing?" whined, the barefoot one.

"Get on! I motioned to him with my gun.

He swung onto the horse's back and just as I was about to let them ride off the tall guy cursed and threatened, "Your old man will pay for this, I'll see to that!"

I grabbed the horse's reins and jerked; His horse reared and dumped him back on the ground.

"What do you know about my Pa?"

"Nothing."

Ma must have looked away from her prisoner, for he kneed his horse, and Ma shouted, "Oh no, you don't, now get off that horse."

"Betty Sue, would you pick up the extra guns and take them to the kitchen?

Without a word, she handed me the gun in her hand, picked up the gun and holster on the ground and the shot gun and preceded to the kitchen.

"What ever you do, Betty Sue, don't fire that shotgun."

Ma moved the muzzle of her rifle, and the man on the horse reluctantly swung down.

"Tie your horse to the wagon wheel and keep on this side where I can see you."

My prisoner started to get up, so I fired a shot right between his ankles, splattering sand in his face.

"I've changed my mind about letting you go. You just stay put and keep your hands where I can see them, you're lucky I'm a poor shot or you'd have a broken leg.

"Mom, can you find me some pigging strings? There should be some on my saddle. We'll just tie these guys up for the sheriff."

"Hey boy, did you ever shoot a man?" called the man on the ground.

I kept my eyes on the other prisoner and watched the speaker out of the corner of my eye.

"I just don't think you have the nerve," he taunted.

Without moving my head, I pointed the gun to a spot between his hand and hip and squeezed the trigger.

"Maybe not but if I keep trying I sure will."

He started to swear, but when I moved the muzzle of the gun, he was looking straight up the barrel. Reaction caused him to crab back a step.

Ma handed Betty Sue the pigging strings and she brought them over. I hand her the gun in my left hand, putting my own back in the holster.

"Keep the gun on him, if he moves shoot." I think we all wondered if she would do it.

After tying slip knots in three of the short ropes used for hobbling a house or tying a calf, I ordered my prisoner to his knees, Slipping a slip knot over his foot, I stood on the rope while putting another slip knot on his wrist, then fashioning another slip knot, I tied his hands together so if he tried to get loose the knots would only pull tighter shutting off the circulation. The third slip knot went around his neck with the two ropes tied together just out of his reach. If he didn't behave, the neck rope would choke him.

"Now get on your horse."

"I can't ride bare back tied up this way."

"You should have thought of that before you tried to bully women and a boy as you called me."

He didn't like the way I mocked him and started to swear again, so I pulled off my bandanna and tied a knot in the middle of it. He clamped his mouth shut, and shook his head.

"Then step on the block of wood and up on the wagon, and keep your mouth shut"

Betty sue brought up his horse again and this time when he stepped on, I quickly cinched his feet together under the horse.

"That should make a bronc rider out of you."

I turned to the second prisoner and there he stood sort of helpless, I'd seen his kind before and could tell he was the kind that would follow a bully, but when the bully was not in charge, he wasn't very brave.

"You don't have to tie me up, I won't do anything."

"I know you won't." I proceeded to tie him just the same as the first one.

While I tied up the second one, Mom had gone to the small pasture where we kept fresh riding stock, and brought back Pa's best riding and roping horse.

Ma tucked the rifle under her arm like she'd done that before, and then leaned over and said something to Betty Sue that I couldn't hear.

Time was wasting so I just rubbed Pa's horse down with a saddle blanket and threw the saddle on him. I wasn't sure that I could tie the lead rope to a horse's tail like I'd heard old ranchers talk about, but I tried it and still wasn't sure, so for safety I took the rope off my saddle and tied it to the lead rope of the horse of the tall prisoner, he was a talker or better said now, a whiner, running the rope through the ring of the lead rope of the middle horse and on up to my saddle horn.

Now gentlemen, this Ol' Bronc is the best roping horse on the place, If you try to run for it, he'll dump the lot of you in one pile, and the way you're tied, I don't think you'd like that.

"I'll get you for this," whined the tall one.

I turned away, and there was Betty Sue with the prettiest smile you ever saw, holding a plate with two roast beef sandwiches and a piece of mince meat pie. I noticed my saddle canteen hanging over her arm with signs that it had just been filled.

I felt kind of foolish, having a pretty young lady watching me eat so I took a sandwich in one hand and fussed with my saddle straps with the other. When it came time for the pie, I had decided that I kind of liked Betty Sue watching, smiled and said, "My favorite," and put away the pie with about six bites.

She just looked over at Ma and smiled. My, she was pretty!

It's a little out of the way, but I'm going to stop by and get Bill Harwood to ride along."

When I swung into the saddle, the big gray wanted to run and I had a hard time holding him. I could hear our tall rider complain, "Whoa there, hold that horse. You want to get us killed?"

You just can't make good time leading horses and less with riders tied up as these were. I sure didn't want to take a chance on stopping to loosen the ropes on their necks. After a while, I began to wonder if that was a mistake, but I wasn't going to stop until we got to Harwood's.

With Bill riding along side to keep watch we decided to untie the rope around their necks. As they tired they had slumped into the ropes that had become almost too tight.

We met the Sheriff and posse at Carl's place. I was glad to give up the prisoners to the posse members who would take them back to town to jail. When I told the sheriff what the man had said about Pa, He asked me a lot of questions. Most of them I couldn't answer.

"You treated 'em mighty rough didn't you? What are you going to tell the judge it they are not guilty?"

"They know something about Pa, or they wouldn't have threatened to kill him."

The sheriff just stood there with a frown on his face.

"Maybe you should ask them some questions?"

"Don't tell me my business!"

"Have you found my Pa yet?"

I didn't mean to, but I sure could disturb that sheriff every time we met.

The sheriff looked at me, and then turned away mumbling something I couldn't hear, and walked over to question the prisoners.

"What do you know about McCloud?"

"This guy is crazy, I don't know anything. We were just looking for work and some grub."

I came up to them just as he said that, and his lying made me angry. I just jerked the rope loose that tied his feet and dumped him on the ground. He lit on his knees and one shoulder.

"Hey there, what are you doing," growled the Sheriff.

"He will talk," My gun slipped unto my hand.

"Sheriff!" he whined.

"You'd better talk!" the Sheriff tightened his jaw, as I'd seen him do before.

Carl come over and looked closely at the other rider. "Wait a minute Sheriff, I know this one. He did some work for me some time back. He was with me when I had a calf fall into the crevice where the wagon was dumped. A stranger in these parts wouldn't know it was there. It's on my place and most of my neighbors don't even know about it."

"Is zat so," the Sheriff looked at the prisoner, who started to nod.

"Keep your mouth shut, we don't know a thing," whined the man on the ground.

"Sheriff," said Carl, "This man's name is Cal Finley, a drifter, and sometimes cowhand."

The sheriff turned his attention to Cal Finley, "you worked for Carl, Here?"

The man Finley only nodded.

"You're the one that knew where to stash the wagon?"

He nodded again.

"What'd you do with the load that was in the wagon?"

Finley only looked at him.

I was getting impatient with the sheriff. I wasn't that interested in the supplies on the wagon right now, I wanted to know where to find Pa.

"Ok, if you won't talk to me, then we we'll find McCloud and then you'll do all your talking before the Judge. He will have no reason to go easy with you. Theft, kidnapping, assault, threatening women, and maybe murder, those are just the charges I can think of right away, if I think on it I might come up with some more.

Now Cal Finley volunteered, "Ross and Jack hid the stuff. We thought we might need it before this was over.

Now I could see that the sheriff knew what he was doing. By not asking directly about Pa, he got the prisoner to talk, which indirectly admitted his guilt, so it would be easier to trick then into telling where Pa was.

I couldn't think of any place for miles where you could hide a man, unless it was with a shovel.

"Where's McCloud:" the sheriff kept working on Cal.

"I don't know! Jack just rode off with him, while Ross and I hauled the wagon up the bluff and dumped it over.

The sheriff turned to the rider I had dumped on the ground, "Your name Ross?

"Sheriff he hurt my back, you gon'na let him get away with that?" He pointed his chin at me.

The sheriff glanced at me then looked back at the man on the ground, "I asked you a question, are you going to answer it?"

"I don't know what these guys are talking about; I'm just a ranchhand looking for work."

The sheriff motioned to his deputy and a posse member, "you two load him up and take these guys in and lock them up."

"Coffee's ready" there stood Mrs. Boucher on the porch with a six quart enamel coffee pot and box full of tin cups. Probably the same one used for round up.

The Sheriff took off his hat and ran his fingers through his hair then put his hat back on and started for the house.

"Sheriff", the whining prisoner begged, "Don't we get some coffee?" We haven't even had a drink of water for three hours"

"Untie them boys they're not going any place. Ya better check them for hidden weapons, first though.

Two of the posse moved over to each prisoner while others watched every move carefully.

After coffee, the deputy took over the supervision of the re-tying of the prisoners and was soon on his way with the help of the appointed posseman.

The Sheriff turned to me, "I don't suppose I could talk you into going home?"

"No Sir."

"I didn't think so." He looked at Carl, who took my defense.

"It seems to me Sheriff that he has proven himself already, and he is a better shot than most of us. He knows the country too."

"Yah, I suppose so," then he addressed everyone and began giving instructions. "You five fan out and head north forming a spoke of a wheel with Sand Creek crossing as the hub. The rest of you divide up and go east and west, space yourselves about three quarters of a mile apart, then move around the clock until you have made a quarter-circle. All of you are packing enough grub for one day. If we don't find anything we will meet back here for water. If you find tracks or something you want help with, use the old Indian trick and run your horse in a circle. Only in an emergency do I want you to fire three shots in rapid succession.

The posse mounted up, and rode off as directed.

"Carl, as soon as you and Rob find some grub to take along we'll get started to the south."

Mrs. Boucher stepped out onto the porch, "I have your lunches ready, some roast beef sandwiches and raw carrots. It's not much, but you fellows have lived on sandwiches before. I'll have a big meal ready for all of you when you get back tomorrow."

I wanted to ride over behind the bluff where we found the wagon, but the Sheriff was sure that the posse going east would do that. We rode down the ranch road together. There wasn't much to say although Carl did remark about no prospects of rain for a day or two.

As we reached the town road, the Sheriff was looking at a small group of trees growing around an outcropping of rock about a half mile due southwest of us. "Let's have a look around that bluff, before we spread out.

The Bandit Bluff was first known as an Indian camp site. Then later on it became notorious for the hiding place of bandits before they robbed the stage at Sand Creek crossing. Rumors lately, were that it was being used again by hold up men, robbing ranchers of their money when they were on their way to town.

As we approached Bandit Bluff the sheriff sent Carl and me to circle around to the north side, while he swung around to the south.

We rode close enough to see through the few trees and could see nothing. Moving right up to the trees, we tied our horses to one and proceeded on foot, carefully examining everything for some sign.

Reaching the south edge of the clump of trees and looking over the fifteen foot drop, we could see the sheriff sitting his horse as if waiting for something to happen.

I moved out into the open and he looked right at me without showing any sign of recognition, then rode up to the south edge of the Bluff.

Carl moved around west of the outcropping of rocks, and approached a secluded spot near the base. The sheriff moved as he watched Carl approaching and signaled that it was all clear.

I sure didn't want to miss anything and didn't waste any time bringing the horses around. Carl and the sheriff were studying carefully what appeared to be an old campfire, but little was left. I began to have more respect for the sheriff as I watched him work. He stood in one spot and studied the detail of every leaf, stick and rock. A less experienced man would have walked around tramping out many of the signs. Finally after some time he looked over at us. "Someone's been here about three, maybe four days ago.

Carl nodded, but I was looking everything over again. There were signs of horses being tied to small trees. The droppings were not fresh, nor were they completely dried out. The grass trampled around a bare spot where a fire had been, was showing signs of springing back and some new growth could be seen which indicated several days had passed since anyone had camped here.

It hadn't rained in a week, so few of the signs had been disturbed. Finally I said, "Sheriff I'd like to take a closer look."

"Sure go ahead; just be careful how you move around."

I looked at every place my foot would step before setting it down. Then I saw it. Just about four feet back from where the fire had been, were two heel marks in the sandy soil, close together as if they had been tied together. The ground had been pushed up as if whoever left these marks had pressed the heels into the ground on purpose to leave a noticeable mark. About the right distance for a big man with hands tied, a patch of grass was pulled out of a place about the size of a man's hand. Then in the center of the space, pressed deep in the soil was the impression of someone's hand. Then in the center of that space, pressed deep in the soil was the impression of someone's left hand.

"Come and see this! Pa left a sign for us." I stood astraddle of the boot marks and pointed to the sandy soil. Pa had lost one half of his ring finger in an old accident. Now he had used this setup of fingers, to leave a different mark on the ground for us to recognize. Only those of us who knew him would notice.

"See these heel marks? He is letting us know that he is tied and held prisoner."

The sheriff came over for a look, "You're ok, kid. But where do we go from here?"

I not only discovered the first tracks, I also discovered why I didn't care for the sheriff's attitude. He didn't respect me as a man. I sensed that, and resented it. Oh well, now that I understood the problem, it made little difference to me what he though. I knew my worth, and also knew I could carry my end of the load and be depended on. Much later, when I was thinking over this discovery, I made a mental note, to never permit disrespect to children or someone younger than I. I would always endeavor to treat them with more respect than they had earned.

While we were there standing over the marks in the sand, I looked up at the sheriff, "From what I know about my father, we should follow a line directed by his boot heels, comparing them to the head of an arrow pointing in a south easterly direction, with the hand print as the base of the arrow.

The Sheriff looking at all points of the terrain, said "Looks like as good a direction as any. I'll ride Rob's arrow and you two fan out, but stay in sight."

We were headed in a direction that would intersect with Sand Creek about a mile down stream. There was nothing in that direction that I could think of but rolling prairie. The Rainy Day Ranch was in that direction about five miles down Sandy Creek. I never could figure why it was called the Rainy Day Ranch, The story was, that Old Grandpa Day, was nick-named Rainy, because he would cloud up like a rainy day when things didn't go right to suit him. Now someone in every generation is call Rainy Day.

Chapter 3

After a day holding up at the Bandit Bluff, Jack began to get nervous. Speaking to no one in general, "This place was too near the main road to town, and one never knew when some outlaw would want to use it for a hide away while waiting for someone to come down the road."

"Something has to be done with all these supplies. There is too much to carry around the prairie on a pack horse." He untied one of McCloud's hands and tied the other behind his back, then held the rifle on him and ordered him to pick up small lime stones twice the size of a mans hand. When they had a considerable pile, Jack shook out a loop and had McCloud step one foot in it. Drawing the rope up tight, he tied the other end to a small tree, untied his other hand, tossed McCloud a shovel, and ordered him to dig a hole about three and a half feet across and four feet deep.

When that was done he had him line the floor and sides with the small stones, lining that with canvas, stored as many of the supplies as it will hold and laid slabs of limestone over the stash, covering it with dirt and sand, and with a limb wiped out the tracks and covered it with leaves.

Without untying his hands, Jack boosted McCloud up on one of the horses of the wagon team. Placing a few supplies that they could use in a pack on the other work horse, and then leading both horses, he headed southeast toward a place on Sand Creek where there was a pool if it wasn't dry. Today it was all dried up.

Jack commented as they rode up to the dried up pool, "Well McCloud, I'll have to tie you while I go to the nearest ranch to fill our canteens and water my horse." He untied the rope that cinched McCloud's feet under the horse, leaving his hands tied together, and then stepped back with his hand to his gun. "Step down and sit over against that tree."

McCloud had no choice, so he followed the instructions. As his captor tied him to the tree, he did his best to make a fist against the tree, trying to keep the rope tight and sat on his hands to hide the fist.

McCloud flinched when Jack grabbed his good hat and beat out the crown, then proceeded to fill it with water from the canteens and water McCloud's team. When the canteens were empty, he threw down the hat, mounted up with a laugh, "Don't go away" and laughed again at his joke, and rode off.

By relaxing his fist McCloud could loosen the rope around the tree, but his wrists were still tied tight. He tried sawing away with the rope against the rough bark of the tree.

Finally, he felt a strand break, He thought, "I must hurry, or I won't have time to get away before he gets back."

By moving from one bark to another he was finally able to get the rope worn through.

"First I must leave a sign." Going over to the sandy edge of the dried up pool he left a mark the he knew Rob could read, but someone that didn't know him would not understand.

Throwing the grub pack on one of his horses, he hurriedly cinched it up Jumping on the other horse he rode bare back toward the Crow's Nest Ranch. There he could get help and a gun. When he met this fellow Jack again He would turn the tables on him and find out what was going on.

Using the heel of his boot he prodded his horse into a rocking horse lope. By loping a while and walking a while, he could make good time over the long haul.

Chapter 4

We had ridden most of the way to the Rainy day Ranch when the Sheriff turned his horse in a tight circle. I was so far away that I couldn't be sure that it was a circle or if he had just reined around to look at something. I decided to turn and ride in his direction, watching him closely to see if his did it again. After riding half of a quarter mile, I decide to ride on and see if he wanted us to come in. We would soon be at the rainy Day Ranch where we could water our horses and fill our canteens.

This was mostly open range country, and as we rode through it I could see little that would help us. We had seen only two trees since leaving the Bandit Bluff, and they were scattered along Sand Creek. There was another tree about a half mile from the Rainy Day Ranch. Sometimes there was a pool of water there but my guess would be that at this time of the year it would be dried up.

Carl and the sheriff were headed for the pool. They would meet a few minutes before me, for I had been riding farther out. The pool must have been dry, for they just sat there waiting for me to come up.

As I rode up I could hear the sheriff asking Carl, What do you make of the scuff marks on that tree?" There were hoof marks all around, but no sign of a fire. "They must have had a cold lunch like we are going to have."

We took a few minutes to read all the signs very carefully. Finally, just as the sheriff went to get his lunch out of his saddlebags, I noticed three holes poked into the sand by the dried up pool. They were positioned in such a way that it could possibly be made by someone's left hand with a missing ring finger. In the place of the ring finger was a scuff mark in the sand where Pa had moved the short finger in a outward motion, pointing toward the east and a little north.

"What do you make of this Sheriff?" I was copying his own words.

The sheriff and Carl came over for a closer look. "Hum'm, what do your think of this Carl?"

Carl looked over at me, "Could be McCloud's mark again"

I looked over at the sheriff, "I think he is telling us that he has gotten untied and is going over to the Crow's Nest Ranch for help. He wouldn't have a gun by this time. And these kidnappers are armed."

The sheriff moved toward his horse, "we can eat while we ride."

We rode together discussing what we thought of the signs left by the dry pool and tree.

"I think," commented the sheriff "that McCloud has the team and the grub and is heading home."

"But Sir," I broke in, "this must have happened several days ago, before I left home looking for him. Why didn't he make it home, and where is he now?"

Now ask me something easy", retorted the sheriff.

We rode on to the Crow's Nest Ranch that was operated by a Mr. Drenon, for investors back east. Three or four miles before we came in sight of the ranch we could see the out cropping of Rocks called "the Crow's Nest". We headed our horses toward the rocks; for we knew that the ranch buildings were nestled in a horseshoe bend of a bluff about a half mile north of the rocks, just across Squirrel Creek.

When we rode over a small rise into the swale, I noticed that only the very tops of the Crow's Nest rocks were in sight.

"Look at that!" The sheriff was pointing to a definite trail where cattle had been driven, because they were bunched together leaving the grass very trampled. "Several head of cattle driven south".

Carl, who had been quiet for some time now, gave his opinion, "There is no market to the south and very few places where a herd of that size could be watered this time of the year."

The sheriff lifted off his hat and wiped the sweat from the hat band. "My guess is that someone wanted McCloud out of the way while they rustled his herd."

"But Sheriff there are cattle all over the range. Why not just take some of each and they wouldn't be noticed for a while?"

"I don't know, maybe they did and McCloud knows something."

I looked over at the sheriff to see what he was driving at, but his face was expressionless.

"Let's ride on over to the Crow's Nest ranch and get some fresh water and see if Drenon knows anything."

Mrs. Drenon met us at the gate, "Drenon isn't home. McCloud come riding in here bare back, leading a pack horse and reported what had happened. Drenon loaned him a cattle horse, and taking a ranchhand, they have gone after cow thieves."

"Rob, we sent a rider to your place to let you know where your Pa is."

"He didn't show up."

"Oh my, I wonder what happened to him, he was one of our best hands."

The sheriff finished watering his horse, and stepped over to us with his take charge attitude. "Ma'am, what time did the men take after the rustlers?"

"That would be three evenings ago."

"Ma'am could we have some fresh horses, at least two, mine is about played out."

"Sure, pick out what you need." She called to an old ranch hand that was puttering around the barn, but keeping an eye on us. "Tex, bring in some good horses for these fellows." Mrs. Drenon returned to the house, to bring us a lunch to take along. We watered our horses again and filled our canteens.

"Carl, someone needs to ride over and round up the posse and bring them over here. Tell them to pick up the trail here and follow as fast as possible. Tex will have extra horses waiting. Each posse man should pick up another horse here and ride hard to catch up. Rob, you ride over and let your mother know what we have found. Your horse is still in good shape, so if I were you, I'd take along your father's team. It will be dark before either of you get home, so keep your eyes open for night riders."

I decided to leave right away instead of picking up the team. We could do that later. The big gray roping horse had covered a lot of miles today, but none of it had been hard riding. So I started him out at a good easy gait and let him set his own pace.

I could be home and back again before Carl got home. It would take a half day to round up the posse, and that might be too late.

We made good time, for there was a good range road between the two ranches, and we didn't have to worry about prairie dog holes.

There was still a light on in our ranch house when I pulled up to the corral, so I hailed the house to let them know who was there. I sure didn't want to face any buck shot. I didn't know what my mother would do, after what happened this morning. I figured she would be more alert to someone coming in late a night.

Mom was very pleased to find out that Pa had been alive three days ago. "Following rustlers can be dangerous, but he can take care of himself."

"Ma, Carl said he would hitch up the buckboard and bring Mrs. Boucher over tomorrow. He said that their milk cow is about dry so he would just turn her out, and that would take care of his chores, till he got back home.

After eating a good meal, I excused myself, "Mom I'm going to take a couple of horses and try to catch up with the sheriff."

"Can't you wait until morning?"

"No, Pa has at least a two day head start and it will take two or three hours to catch the Sheriff."

As I gathered up more shells for my guns Betty Sue came over and laid a hand on my arm, Rob, be careful."

The tone of her voice make me not want to leave, I turned and looked her right in the eye, something I don't think I had ever done before. I wanted to reach out to her, but somehow I was just too shy. I knew what I had to do, I must ride back. There would be no stopping until we found Pa, and brought back the stolen herd.

Smiling at Betty Sue, I squeezed her hand and gathered up the grub Ma was putting together. With a shy "see you later", I started to the corral, to find my big sorrel and the black of Carl's. These two horses got along well together, so we started down the trail running side by side.

When we came to the bend in the road that crossed Sand Creek and went up to the Crows Nest Ranch house, I turned toward the southwest across the prairie to where we had seen the cow trail.

Even though the moon had come up, I had to slow down so I could tell when we were coming up on a prairie dog town. I couldn't lose either one of these good horses to foolish riding in the dark.

The slower pace gave me more time to think. Moving cattle would need water. They could not stop at ranches for water. There was one windmill with two tanks on the Crow's Nest Range about three miles south, but they would have been there at least three days ago. They would not be able to move toward the river that followed the mountain range, for there would be too many ranch houses located along the river. That size herd could never be watered there without notice.

Before long, I decided that I had made a mistake leaving the range road, which was little more than a trail, but it could be faster traveling at night. To move a herd without being seen, they would have to move it at night and let it scatter in the day light.

Someone who knows where all the watering places are would be leading this herd. Before long, I came across a regularly used wagon trail heading south. I knew the herd had three or more day's head start, so I turned onto the wagon trail and gave my horse his head. He set a good pace in one wheel track, while the black came alongside in the other. About an hour down the trail, we came to a small creek. Not taking any chances, I brought the horses to a walk at the crossing.

The black pulled to the right and I let my horse follow. There was a faint smell of water, and burnt wood. I let the horses drink. Just then a voice from a clump of trees by the water hole commanded, "I have a gun leveled at your middle, don't move a muscle."

"Dan", I said to my horse, "I do believe the sheriff has a problem. I wonder if he is all alone out here."

"All right, Kid, you can get down." "Where do you think you're going? I thought I sent you home."

"I've been home Sheriff, I gave the news about Pa, and rode out again."

"Hum-mp. Well now that you're here, you might as well get some sleep. We'll start at day light."

"Sheriff, the way I figure, if I were moving stolen cattle across the country, and didn't want anyone to see me, I'd move them at night. Then at daylight I'd find a lonesome spot and let the herd spread out. That wouldn't look so suspicious. I think I'll just ride the wagon trail till morning and circle around to see if I can find their tracks."

"You've got me all awake, now, so if you'll rest a bit while I saddle up, I'll go along with you.

"I dismounted, and walked around a little, to relax my saddle muscles, then switched my saddle to the black.

I could hear the sheriff muttering as he stumbled around, breaking camp and saddling his horse. His borrowed horses were not used to him and gave him some trouble in the dark.

Finally, as he rode out of the shadows into the moonlight at the crossing, I swung unto the saddle and led the way down the trail.

The sheriff was not used to having someone else taking the lead, and I could hear him muttering something about impertinent young whippersnapper.

It was a long, lonely ride at night. We stopped several times and switched horses, making very good time. I guessed that we traveled twice as far as they could move cattle at night.

When morning came we decided to let out horses rest and graze, while we cooked up some coffee and breakfast.

We gathered cow chips for fire and while the sheriff made the coffee, I fried some bacon and made sandwiches. The Sheriff tried one and remarked, "Not bad, if we had an egg to go with them."

"Sheriff you've been spending too much time in town. You're losing your taste for the good ol' range food."

He gave me a crooked smile, and continued eating like he hadn't eaten much last night. "Riding all night gives a man an appetite"

I stretched out, and tipped my hat over my eyes. The sheriff poured another cup of coffee and sat sipping at it as if in deep thought. When I awoke, the horses were standing with head lowered as if they were sleeping. When I moved over to unhobble my horses, the sheriff moaned and got up from the ground as if he were stiff and lame. He gathered up his horses and we saddled up without much conversation.

Then as we swung into the saddles he looked over the horizon and said, "Which way do you want to go? Remember our signal."

Without a word I reined my horse to the left, and he rode to the right. We both rode in a southerly direction.

As my route was up grade, I didn't hurry my horses. When we topped the grade, and dropped out of sight of the sheriff, I began to wonder if I was riding to far, but it paid off, for just over the hill, out of sight of the trail, I found what we were looking for. There were signs of a herd of cattle being moved.

I rode back to the top of the hill and was making the third circle before the sheriff signaled that he had seen me. Needing to save my horses I waited for him. When I noticed that he was angling south, I started moving slowly in that direction, stopping once in a while to let my horses graze.

When we came together, I explained to the sheriff what I had found. He must have been getting tired, for he just nodded and angled toward the cattle's trail.

The terrain was more rolling here than in Squirrel Creek valley where we first found the trail of stolen cattle, Just as we topped a rise, we spotted a man on foot, very carefully picking his way through the sage brush, As we came up to him, he stood very still, with gun in hand ready to shoot.

The sheriff appeared to be unconcerned about the gun, "Where's you horse?"

"Sheriff, a big guy, about six-two, slipped up on me in the night, took my horse and my boots."

"We can't leave you out here afoot, take my extra horse."

The sheriff swung his horses around so that the young man could mount, making sure that they were between us.

As the stranger mounted the bare-back horse, he straightened up looking right down the barrel of my six gun; then he looked at the sheriff, who was holding his gun on him too.

"What's this? You guys working with this horse thief?"

"Maybe so, we sure aren't working for cattle rustlers." I relieved him of his hand gun, he had no rifle.

"What do you mean, Sheriff?" We were just moving some cattle for someone in town,"

"Stolen cattle?

"I don't know anything about stolen cattle. Noland told me that the boss wanted some cattle moved to a range down in New Mexico. Didn't say nothing about stolen cattle."

The young thief looked younger than I, and as I looked him over, I could tell that he was no cowhand.

"You come far looking for work?" I butted in.

"Yaw, this was the first job I could find between here and Missouri."

"Who hired you?"

"This guy by the name of Noland, I never heard any other name for him."

"Do you know who you are working for?"

"No, Noland did talk about someone he called the Boss."

"Didn't you think it strange that you moved cattle only at night?"

"I complained about that and someone said it was because of the heat."

"How many men are there, driving this herd?"

"There were four, but the other night, a fellow they called Moose, just didn't show up, come daylight."

"The sheriff chuckled, "Maybe he lost his horse and boots too."

"It sounds as if Pa has caught up with the rustlers and is cutting them down to size."

The sheriff tossed the lead rope to the young captive and warned, "If you know what is good for you, you'll keep up."

I leaned over and tied the lead rope back into the halter, so it could be used like reins, and we rode off to catch up with the sheriff.

I was wishing that I had changed horses, for now that the sheriff had only one horse he would not be stopping to change horses. We had been riding pretty hard, so when the sun was high in the sky, we stopped for lunch and warmed up some coffee, while the horses rested. I took the time to change saddles on my horses.

It wasn't until about sundown that we heard gun shots just over the rise. I began to have more respect for the sheriff, when I saw him at work. First he tied the would-be cowboy's feet. Then with an eight foot tether rope, he tied the horse to the prisoner's feet. This puzzled me for a time until I turned around just as we were leaving and saw the young fellow try to get up and hobble over to the horse. Just as soon as he jumped a step forward, the horse shied away and sat him down again on his bill fold.

The sheriff chuckled, "He won't try that too many times in a day."

As we topped the rise the gun fire increased, it sounded as if someone was pinned down. Someone was lying in the sage about a hundred yards to the left. Two horses were hobbled near a wash that was just about knee deep. Our horses were still not in sight of the men in the washout when we dismounted. I dropped the lead rope on the black, hoping she would stand ground tied. I hoped that my horse would come if I called him. Most of the time he would, unless we were on home range, then you could never tell.

We lifted our rifles from the saddle boots and Injun'd up through the sage, to a place where we could see the rustlers plainly. There was no place for them to hide from our position.

"Now let's see if you can shoot as good as they say you can."

I don't know if the sheriff was being good to me or just making fun, but I didn't really care. I lifted my rifle and sighted at a spot where I thought the first man's gun should be, and squeezed the trigger, and automatically levered in another shell.

The man let out a yell and hunkered down bumping into his partner.

"This is the sheriff! Throw your guns out and come out with you hands up." When the sheriff wanted to, he could make himself heard half across the prairie.

No one moved, "Put another shot right behind them."

I pointed close behind them hoping to splatter them with sand. It worked, for when the sand hit the back of their necks they knew we could see them, and there was no place to go.

The sheriff stood up, "Keep them covered McCloud," he shouted, and then to me, "I'll keep out of your line of fire. If they move, you'll have to shoot 'em. Can you do that?"

I nodded, but inside I wasn't sure, so I sighted in on their knees, I didn't want to kill any one. But at this distance I could make sure that they didn't ride horses for a long time.

I held my breath, then I had to tell myself to relax. I saw the one on the other side drop his hand just a little and stop. I estimated the spot where his right elbow would be and squeezed. He spun around and fell. The Sheriff shot while he was walking and missed, but kept walking. "Good shooting, son. Come on down McCloud. Rob you stay put and keep us covered."

Out of the corner of my eye, I could see Pa standup and start toward the sheriff. I kept my rifle sighted on the rustlers. The sheriff stood with his gun drawn while Pa walked up to him.

"Come on in Rob. Bring the horses."

My horse had never liked gunfire so had shied back about a hundred feet. I walked over to the black and called, "Come here Dan." As I picked up the lead rope on the black and began to pet her neck, my horse trotted up with his head to one side, dragging the reins. When he put his head over my shoulder, I scratched his neck, "I think you're jealous." I swung into the saddle and rode over to the sheriff's horse, gathered up the reins and started down the grade.

The thieves were tied up and the sheriff was trying to bandage up the busted elbow of the tall one, who looked at me with a look of hate that had murder mixed with it.

I looked him right in the eyes, shook my head and said "You were told not to move". I could see that didn't change things with him. We all knew that even with the proper medical attention, he might not be able to draw with that arm again.

"You were lucky", said the sheriff with compassion, "If it was anyone else that had pulled that trigger. You'd be dead."

Pa stepped over and patted me on the back, I tipped my hat a said, "We missed ya, Pa."

"I knew you'd come looking, but there for a minute, I thought I would have to shoot both of them to get our cows back."

"Our cows?"

"Yes son, those are Circle M cows out there."

I looked around at the cattle scattered over several acres and wondered how many were out of sight over the hills, for cows can move a long way in a day.

Pa and I checked the saddles on the prisoners horses, Packed up their bedrolls and camp equipment, When I rode up to pick up Pa's horse, I noticed that he now had three horses hobbled and two with saddles. My guess was that the third one was Missouri's horse.

When we mounted up, the thief with the busted elbow was in so much pain, that he slumped over in the saddle. I could tell that he hurt more with every step of the horse.

As we backtracked to pick up our first captive, we were all so tired from our sleepless nights that we almost missed the humor of the sight before us. For there sat Missouri on his tied hands with his feet held in the air with the bug eyed horse pulling back hard on the tether rope. Every time Missouri would try to get his feet on the ground, the horse would step back and jerk his head up, sliding Missouri through the sage. Finally, when we rode up, there stood the horse with both eyes bulging with fear and front legs wide, bracing against the pull of the rope.

"Son", the sheriff observed, as he untied Missouri's feet and letting him stand up, "Sometimes the harder we fight against life, the harder life becomes."

Missouri was acting like such a green horn that I was beginning to believe his story. "Sheriff, I think I believe Missouri's tale about coming out here looking for work. I don't think he knew that they were stealing the cattle."

Missouri shook his head.

"Your name Noland?" the sheriff turned to the cow hand with the broken elbow.

He winced and nodded his head.

"Tell me the truth. Did this fellow know you were stealing cattle?"

"Maybe not, but he should have guessed it, if he wasn't such a green horn. We just told him that we were moving cattle to another range. He was new and we couldn't trust him not to turn us in."

The look that Missouri gave the sheriff was full of questions.

"He could help me round up the cattle while Pa helps take the rustlers in."

"I suppose so, if he will promise to come for court, when I need him." Then looked at him with a frown.

"I, ah, yes sir! I'll be there, just you say when,"

"I'll let you know, just don't let me down or I'll put out a wanted poster on you."

Pa agreed with the plan and suggested that we take the food and water with us, and drive the extra horse back with the herd.

With this last suggestion, Missouri acted for the first time like he had a new lease on life, He dusted himself off with his hat. Then rubbing the circulation back into his wrists, asked if he could have his gun back.

Reaching into his saddle bags, the sheriff took out the gun that we had taken from this green horn. Looking it over carefully, he opened it up and shook out the shells and then handed it to Missouri. "Don't load it until you are out around the cows and out of my sight." Then as a second thought he reached into the saddle bag again, "Your gun uses the same shells as mine, and it looks as though you are about out. Take this handful just in case."

Missouri holstered the gun and pocketed the shells. Then looking mighty pleased, he caught up his horse. We loaded all the food into our saddle bags and in the bed roll behind my saddle. Most of the remaining water was poured into our canteens, for they would soon be at a ranch where they could refill.

Missouri looked up with a lopsided grin, and we began to pick our way through the sage toward the herd.

As the sheriff and Pa rode off with the prisoners, the Sheriff began to question. What happened to Drenon and his cow-hand?"

McCloud began to explain, "When we came upon the first night rider, off by himself, there was gun play. Drenon was wounded and I sent them back. Drenon would need help, for their prisoner was the hold up man named Jack that had held me captive; He was also wounded in the shoot out."

"We must have missed them when we rode all night."

"They probably rode straight for the Crows Nest Ranch to get there as fast as possible.

"What happened to the other one of the four rustlers?"

"If he didn't walk out to the nearest ranch, we should come up on him sometime tomorrow. I led his horse for a half a day before I turned him loose. He acted sort of mean, so I left him without a gun or boots, just in case he came upon an unsuspecting rider and want his horse."

The Sheriff turned to Noland, who was swaying in the saddle with pain. "Looks like we have you all rounded up. Don't suppose you want to tell me who your boss is?" It sure would be a shame to have you go to jail, and let him off scott free."

The wounded prisoner only shook his head, tipping it toward the busted arm, as if to try to ease the pain,

The sheriff tried again, "We are about two, maybe three days to a doctor. You could lose that arm if we can't find you some medicine you could die of blood poisoning. Is it worth that to cover for someone who is not going to pay you anyway?"

"Oh, leave me alone!"

"O.K., I don't care if you want to face the judge alone. You are just lucky, that McCloud here didn't want to hang you on the spot."

The prisoners refused to talk, riding with heads down and some times with eyes closed.

"It's going to be getting dark soon. I suppose we should camp on the rim, so if any of the posse is catching up, they can see our fire."

They picked a spot on the rim that could be seen from the northwest. Pa took great care to see that the sage brush was pulled in a very wide circle, so no sparks would start a prairie fire. The only thing to burn was a few cow chips and sage brush. Both could send sparks flying for several feet.

When he helped his prisoners down from their horses, the sheriff looked at Noland's bandages, and shook his head. "You're going to bleed to death if we keep riding, unless I can tie off the upper arm to stop the bleeding." He took a bandanna and tied a knot in the center then placed the knot on the inside of the upper arm, and twisted it until Noland groaned, then tied a double knot to hold it on. "We'll put a sling on the arm tomorrow."

Chapter 5

Missouri and I rode hard to round up the herd before dark. Fortunately, for several nights they had been rounded up every evening for a night drive, and they were getting used to the round-up. By the time night began to close in around us, we had closed the circle and reduced it to the smallest size. We moved them a little toward the north and let them bed down for the night.

We met on the south side of the herd when it was almost dark. "Missouri, you sure wouldn't run out on me and leave me to hold this herd together alone?"

"Hey, I'm no out law, but if I run now I would be, and the chance of living it down would be a slim one."

I squirmed around in the saddle until I could see into the saddle bags where I knew we had placed some dried beef. "Here, chew on a hand full of this, I think we should keep circling the herd for a while then we will take turns getting some rest."

Missouri took the handful of beef jerky, and with one in his mouth and the rest in his shirt pocket, he started around the herd. I did the same, with the thought that this kind of a meal would put a heavy demand on our water supply. Oh well, tomorrow when the herd was moving, one of us could go after water, if the water tank that we should reach early in the day was too dirty to drink.

About an hour after dark, the herd was bedded down, so I let Missouri take the first watch, and tethered my horse. Using my saddle for a pillow, I rolled out my bed roll and stretched out within the circumference of the horse's tether rope. I knew he could smell a sidewinder, and if one came by, his snort would wake me. I had slept this way before and was not afraid to sleep under his feet if necessary. Many a time I have been awakened when sleeping this way, with my horse's nose in my face, or nudging my arm.

The first thing I remembered was a loud snort right over my head and someone with a loud whisper saying, "Rob, Hey Rob! I can see your horse, but it's too dark to see you.

"It's okay Missouri, I think I'm right under his head."

"I can't tell the time but it's so dark I can't see the herd any more. The last time around I thought I would not find my way back."

I felt like I hadn't slept for days. I woke up just enough to tell Missouri to bed down till morning. When Ol' Dan nudged me awake, it was well on the way to getting light and the cattle were up and moving around, starting to spread out to graze.

I looked over at Missouri, and he had bedded down well back from his horse. Now that's something only a green horn would do out here. Sure enough, we had a camp visitor. Now maybe you have heard stories about rattlesnakes not being out at night, but don't believe it for one minute. For there was Missouri, on his back, with his head propped on his saddle.

On his chest was a granddaddy prairie rattler looking him right in the nose. Moving his head back and forth with every snore Missouri made. I was sure glad that Missouri was asleep. Without getting up I pulled my six gun from under the edge of my saddle. When I did, the rattler sensed movement, and raised his head and held still like he was trying to listen. That was all I needed, I drew a tight bead on his head and fired. Missouri jumped like he had been shot. He reached around to find his misplaced gun and put his hand right in the middle of the dead rattler, and let out a Missouri yell that almost stampeded the cattle. If they had been more wild, they would have. He was on his feet now and twenty feet away.

"Stand still, will ya, there might be another one around",

although I doubted it. For if there had been with all this commotion, it would have rattled it's tail off. In all the excitement, I couldn't help being full of mischief.

"Hey, Missouri, where there is one, there are always two."

Now that is an old tale that I had never found to be true, but it worked, for Missouri was standing as if he would bolt and run at the first warning. He looked that sage over as if he was sure that it was crawling.

When I doubled up laughing he came back very slowly without taking his eyes off the ground.

"I thought you were shooting at me."

I couldn't stop laughing long enough to answer.

He looked the rattler over from a distance. "You blew his head right off.

"I had to, He was on your chest trying to figure out what makes a man snore."

For the first time this morning, he looked right at me. If I ever saw a man look scared near death, I was seeing one now.

"You know Missouri, this is a big one. If we can get a fire going we could roast him for breakfast."

His face went white as death, and he just looked at me. I thought he was going to be sick, but after a little he picked up his saddle and said, "I don't want any breakfast."

Now I was sorry I'd scared him so much, for I sure would like to start what I knew was a long day with some coffee.

It was my turn to be embarrassed. I just stood there trying to find words to say, while he saddled up and rode off around the herd.

As I looked after him, I though, "He'll make a good hand. In fact, he was now, for he seemed to like cattle and knew how to handle them. Although he had said that he had not handled this large a herd before, he still knew cattle.

Ol' Dan was waiting for me to share a little of my water with him so after he was saddled, I did. Then we rode out to give Missouri a hand. The next few days would be a long hot, hard drive.

Chapter 6

About the third day, just after high noon, the air became charged with electricity and both cows and horses became nervous. I rode over to Missouri and motioned to him while I took off my shirt and stuffed it into my hat. At first he thought I was crazy, but then it started to hail, with just a few hail stones the size of walnuts. Only a few hit the ground before he ripped off his shirt and stuffed it into his hat. Then when I unrolled my ground sheet and blanket and wrapped them over my back and arms, He did the same.

Soon the hail came faster, but thankfully smaller. It still was it pounded our backs through the canvas. Walnut size hail was breaking the skin on our horses and streaks of blood were running down their sides. The wind come at us from the north, making the cattle bunch up with heads down. They moved with the wind. Our horses would not face the wind and hail, and the best we could do was to try to slow the cattle down as we slowly lost ground, which would have to be made up after the storm. It only lasted about an hour and a half. The tough part was not being able to find any type of shelter that far out on the range.

Even though it was the twenty-fourth of July, the hail piled up three or four inches on the ground, making it look and feel like winter. I had heard of this kind of storm but had never seen one.

When the storm was over, the sun came out so bright that the white of the hail almost blinded us. It seemed to me that the sun was laughing in our faces.

During most of the storm, Missouri's horse was acting like a wild bronc, and Missouri wound up with most of the bruises, but we both had lumps. We took all the time needed to rub our horses down with hail to wash off the blood stains.

The cattle were battered, but there was nothing we could do for them, except start them moving in the right direction. We decided to make double time to warm them up and make up the miles lost in the storm.

It wasn't long before we begun to notice jackrabbits lying dead under the hail. Just before the storm, the jackrabbits were plentiful. Now as we moved the herd along, we didn't see any live ones.

In two or three hours, with the sun shining, the hail was mostly melted and water was running in every little stream. In a few days, as we returned to Squirrel Creek Valley, we could see signs of water marks high along the creek bed, although the water was gone except for a few pools along the creek.

We moved the cattle over the rise to the back side of the Crow's nest rock east of the ranch buildings. If we held a course straight north, we would drop right into the bend in Squirrel Creek where there would be plenty of water after the rain.

When we drove up to the creek, the lead cows shied away from something washed up against a curve in the creek bank.

"Ride in close Missouri, and move them farther north, there is more water there anyway."

He rode in swinging his rope, with a voice that carried much greater threat than the rope. He tried driving the herd back from the creek so they could more easily negotiate the bend.

As the herd began to move, Missouri rode over to let his horse drink. I looked up just in time to see him jerk his horse's head up, almost setting him down. When the horse had calmed, he stood in the saddle for a better look at something washed up against the opposite bank.

"Come over here, Rob."

In a few hops of my horse, I reined in beside him.

"Look over there," It was a awful sight, some poor cowhand looked like he had been under the high water and washed down stream lodged against the bank and partly covered with clutter.

"You reckon he drowned?"

"We'll have to get him out and haul him in some way."

I was riding the black and she didn't want to get any closer, so I handed the reins to Missouri and waded across to the body, I wasn't halfway to it, when I recognized him as the Crow's Nest rider.

There was something funny about his position that puzzled me.

"Hey, Missouri, he's been shot right through the wish bone", I looked closer. "Twice"

Missouri dismounted and come over for a better look. "I believe he was buried here before the storm and hasn't changed his position."

"Yeah, looks like several days, and the water hasn't helped much either."

I walked over to my horse and untied my pack, shook out the ground sheet and carried it over and covered up the body. It wouldn't be much help in keeping away the varmints, but I felt better about it.

It was a couple of weary, stiff riders that left the cattle on the range above our ranch and rode for home.

When we rode into our ranch, the sheriff had already met the posse and returned to town with the prisoners. Pa came out of the barn and gave us the information, and I told him about the dead cowhand.

For a while he just stood there looking at me, "We covered the ground between here and the ranch looking for him before the storm."

Pa still looked a little shocked. In all our years in the west nothing like this had happened to us before.

I spoke up, "It looked as if whoever did this, dumped him in the creek and caved dirt over him, but all this water washed it off."

I was so tired, that all I wanted to do was to find a comfortable place to sleep. We must have looked tired, for Pa talked us into going to the house to get something to eat and to rest, while he hooked up the team to go get the body.

I noticed as I handed him the horse and turned to go that he had the wagon box almost repaired.

"Say Rob, Betty Sue is still here, Her Pa thought it best she didn't ride with the sheriff and prisoners, besides I believe you have something of hers."

I turned and looked at the black mare, and all of a sudden I wasn't felling as tired as before.

"Come on Missouri, let's get something to eat."

As we came up to the house, I began to realize how dirty I was. A little range dirt hadn't bothered me before, but now it didn't feel right for Betty Sue to see me this dirty. We headed for the back door where I knew we would find a pail of water and soap. At least I could get my face, arms and hands clean.

We could hear mother in the kitchen, and I knew she was warming up a good meal. I was sure that Missouri's first meal in her house would be a good one.

We entered the house to a hearty, "Hi Rob".

It was all I could do to look at Betty Sue. She looked so fresh and beautiful. I was more conscious that I needed a shave and that I had been in the same clothes for several days, out on the dusty prairie.

"Hi Betty Sue, Mom, this is Missouri, ah, any way that's what I call him, he's from Missouri."

Mon was always polite, to all our guest, "Hello Missouri".

"My name is Wayne, Ma'am." We all looked at him for this was the first time any of us had heard his name. We sat down to the table while Mom and Betty

Sue set the food on. It looked like enough to feed every one on a roundup, but when we were through with it there wasn't enough to feed a pet dog.

Missouri must have been a mind reader, or had sixth sense or something, for when we got up from the table he said. "I'll go help your Pa, you can stay here."

Then Ma looked at me; I knew I had to tell her.

"We found the body of the Crow's Nest cowhand, down by the creek."

"Was it old John that was sent here with a message?"

"Yes."

She turned to the stove, and the look on Betty Sue's face was a look of sorrow, and sympathy in her eyes, I thought I could see a compassion for me. Whatever the look, it made me want to reach out for her. Now we had been good friends, but I never felt quite like this before. The feeling didn't last long, for all of a sudden, I felt very tired and weary.

I helped myself to warm water from the tank on the side of the stove and filled a large pan that I took to my room.

After washing up, I slipped between clean sheets and stretched out on my bed. Now I enjoyed sleeping out on the Prairie, but there is nothing like your own bed.

When I woke up, it was morning, and all of a sudden I began to feel ashamed, I should have slept in the bunk house. Because of my thoughtlessness, Betty Sue would have had to sleep on the cot in the living room.

The more I thought about it, the longer it took me to dress and the longer it took, the more I couldn't think what to say. Finally I forced myself into the kitchen.

"Hey, I'm sorry; I should have slept in the bunk house. I just wasn't thinking." I looked into the living room and there, as I somehow knew they would be, all the blankets were folded neatly at the head of the cot. "Hey, I'm sorry".

Betty Sue put her hands on her hips and scolded, "Rob McCloud! I'll hear no more of your sorrys. You needed your sleep, I got along fine." One look at her and I felt fine too. I didn't know what to say, so I just smiled and sat down to breakfast. Now I couldn't think of anything to say but, I did a lot of thinking anyway. This girl sure had spirit. I had seen last night, that she felt compassion and sympathy, now I could see another good quality, spirit. I knew right then that I liked having this girl in my house.

Pa came in from outside, about that time. He usually did some chores before breakfast. He would often say, "Sunrise is the best time of the day." I'm not sure I always agree with that, for I usually wake up very slowly. It sometimes takes quite some time for me to begin to enjoy the day.

"Well, Rob, Missouri hired on with the Crow's nest Ranch.

With old John gone they were short of a hand. He'll be treated well there, and if he works hard, the job will last as long as he needs it."

"He's a good worker, and good with cattle," I added.

"After breakfast, Rob, you had better saddle up Betty Sue's horse and see that she gets home safely." He looked over at Betty Sue, "I suppose you're anxious to get home."

"Oh, not really. It has been fun here helping Mother McCloud." She looked at Ma as if they knew something we didn't. I had never heard her call my Mom, Mother before, and wondered if it had some hidden meaning.

I got up from the table, "I can be ready any time you are."

"Okay Rob, as soon as I help with the dishes"

"Oh go ahead, I can get the dishes, there aren't many." My Mother never wanted to be obligated to anyone.

"That's okay, Rob can bring up the horses."

I stepped out the back door, looking over at the horse pasture, where we had fenced off a quarter section, for the horses we used regularly, an whistled a special whistle that sometimes called up my big sorrel. He looked up, but kept on eating. The second time I whistled both he and the black looked up and started toward the gate. Ol' Dan wouldn't be outdone, and broke into a run. Soon all the horses were coming in on the run, I got the gate opened just in time, but closed it right behind the black and let the rest of the horses circle out and look on.

Dan and the black circled the corral a couple of times while I opened the barn door for Dan's stall. He had always had a double stall, and had not had to share it very often. Most of the time he was never tied in the barn, I would just shut him in the stall, and he would never share the stall with any horse without being tied. This time he didn't seem to mind, as long as the black kept her head out of his feed box.

I went around to the feed barrel where we kept a bait of oats and gave him some, because he would have a hard days ride. It didn't seem fair, so I gave the black some too. Then Ol' Dan, true to nature, left his feed box and tried to eat hers, too. When I scolded him, he laid his ears back, but returned to his own box of grain.

I saw no reason to tie either horse, and began to rub them down and saddle them while they ate. No use trying to tighten the cinches, until we were ready to ride.

I hung the bridles on the saddles and was looking for a fresh ground sheet and blanket, when Pa opened the barn door. He helped with the black's bridle and we started for the house.

"Son, that Betty Sue is a fine girl; you see that you treat her like it. Our families have been friends for a long time."

"Sure Dad, I was just reading in the Scripture the other day, how Christ takes care of the Church like a man should his bride, so she can be presented to him as a bride without spot or wrinkle."

Pa reached over and patted me on the back and said, "You'll do okay, son. You just be faithful to God, and you'll not be let down."

Now Pa didn't come right out and say what he meant, but we both understood clearly, and I think he understood that I thought Betty Sue would make a good wife.

Pa handed me a five dollar gold piece and said, "You'd better go on into town and let the sheriff know what happened to Old John."

Betty Sue was waiting for us, dressed in jeans, boots and hat, as we led the horses up to the front porch. Pa tightened the black's cinch while I took care of my own saddle. Then, being gallant as he was, Pa held his hands on his knee while she stepped in and was lifted to a mounting position. I could see that she had mounted this horse hundreds of times by herself, but she nobly accepted Pa's help, with one of her big smiles, then looked at me with a nod. I accepted the signal and we waved at the folks and cantered down the lane to the ranch road. Then I think because we were both a little embarrassed at our first ride together, when we turned onto the ranch road, we let our mounts run a ways. Even though they were running out full length neither tried to out run the other. At last, we pulled them up, and laughed at each other. Betty Sue patted the black on the neck and laughingly said, "I don't think either wanted to win."

"That black sure proved to be some horse this last week."

"I knew she would. My daddy let me train her myself. She does well, for a three year old, doesn't she?"

"She can keep up with Ol' Dan here; they make quite a team."

Betty Sue looked away, then out over the prairie, like she wanted to change the subject.

As we rode along without talking, I looked over at Betty Sue several times, she always looked happy, and when our eyes met, she never gave me one of those, "I'm embarrassed" grins, but always a pleasant "all is well, I'm happy to be here" look.

It was about a three and a half hour ride from out ranch to the Bouchers, and I for one was glad she didn't feel the need to make conversation all the time. We had ridden for about half an hour without talking, when she turned to me with, "I would like to hear about your adventure."

Now I was never a hand at talking to young ladies. For some reason, I could never think of anything to say, but spinning a tall tale, I was good at that! Although I'm ashamed to admit, that I can sometimes embellish them just a little too much.

Anyway, I started at the beginning and told her the whole story. When I told about my narrow escape in town, she gasped. About finding the wagon, she frowned in a sweet proud way, and when I told about finding the sheriff. She smiled, but when I described tying Missouri's feet to the lead rope of a spooky horse, she giggled. When I got to the shooting of the rustler in the elbow, became very sad and asked if I thought he would bleed to death.

I replied, "It might be better that hanging," Then I wished I hadn't said that, for all she said was, "Rob!..?

So I went into great detail about finding Missouri hanging by his feet from a frightened horse and she laughed right out loud, with the prettiest sorrowful grin on her face. "Was he hurt?"

"No, just his pride, and that didn't last long when the sheriff turned him loose to help with the herd."

She must have been thinking about it later, for she burst out laughing, Then she looked at me and said, "Sometimes I wish I could ride with you guys, you have so much excitement.

I tipped my head to look at her under the rim of my hat, and she reached out and knocked my hat up so she could see my face. "Don't be silly, I know it wouldn't work, but we girls miss all the excitement."

"Yeah, I know", I replied, "like holding up a poor helpless cowhand with a double barreled shot gun. After all, he was just looking for work".

"Oh, you!" She kicked out with a foot in the stirrup and missed me, but hit my horse in the ribs. He broke into a dead run so fast, that I almost lost my hat.

I let him run for a while, and then pulled him up a little to let the black catch up. Then I reached out and patted Dan on the neck, and said so that Betty Sue could hear; "I didn't do it Dan, it was the mean ol' people we ride with."

Betty Sue chimed in, "I'm sorry Dan, but that mean ol' rider of yours had it coming!" We both laughed.

We hadn't ridden long when Betty Sue broke the silence, with, "Rob, do you have any plans for the future?"

With all this joking I was feeling rather bold and replied, "Oh, I thought once that I'd maybe come a courtin', but it's such a long ways to go for such things."

"Robert McCloud, you stop that or I'll never, ever ride with you again."

"Would you if I did?"

"Did what?"

"Ride over to see you some time."

She looked at me as if she was trying to decide, "Are you serious about that?"

"What?"

"About coming over just to see me?"

"Well, I might see your Dad while I was there."

"Rob, you stop teasing or I might say no."

"Then that means yes?"

She nodded, with such a tender look that I nudged my horse with my left heel that she couldn't see, and pretended to busy myself with my active horse.

"Rob, you are welcome to come as often as you like."

I nodded. "Maybe, when I get back from town."

"Are you going on to town?"

"I need to report old John's death to the Sheriff."

"Oh I wish I could go with you."

"It's a long hot dusty ride, down and right back."

"With you, it wouldn't be long, it would be fun."

I could feel my ears getting red on the tops. I was sure glad they were shaded by my hat.

We were too happy to be tired from the long ride and soon we were on the hill overlooking Sand Creek Valley. Over to the right, a little over a half mile, was the Boucher's ranch.

"Isn't that a beautiful sight?"

With a little nudge Ol' Dan stepped side ways until we almost bumped. I reached out my hand and she took it for just a moment, and answered, "The whole world looks beautiful."

"I know."

She was still smiling as we rode down to the ranch.

Mrs. Boucher must have seen us coming, but she didn't come our on the porch until we rode right up to the step.

Betty Sue slipped down and bounded up on the porch without a sign of having ridden almost three and one half hours. She gave her mother a big hug, "Oh it is so good to be home, but I did have such a good time with Mrs. McCloud. She is so understanding and nice to work with, it was just a pleasure every day."

Her mother raised her eyebrows, as if to say, "My little girl is growing up."

Carl came up just then and Betty Sue gave him a welcome that any father would enjoy. I don't know why, but I was very happy with the way Betty Sue greeted her folks I kind of thought, that if I were a father, that was the way I would want my daughter to treat me.

Both of her folks seemed to find joy in the way she was acting. "Come on in Son, and have a bite with us before you go." Carl put a hand on my shoulder, "Mom's been watching that road for two days, expecting you to come riding in."

Mrs. Boucher just smiled, put her arm around Betty Sue, and led the way into the house. "You men get cleaned up", she chuckled, "I started lunch when

I saw you stop on the top of the hill. Lunch will be ready when you are".

Carl and I went out and tied the horses where they had access to water at the windmill, then went around the house to the wash bench at the back door. When we came back in, the table was set with food fit for a king. That is just what Carl said.

Just then from the stairway came a voice, "Or fit for a queen". I looked up to see a fresh and beautiful young lady that was feeling good about our ride home. I guess I was hoping that our new found friendship was what made her feel like a queen.

As we sat down Betty Sue exclaimed, Mom! Dad! They found Old John, shot." She looked at me for help, so I told that part of the story and finished by saying I was on my way to let the Sheriff know.

After lunch, Carl suggested that I would make better time if I would take his best saddle horse and let mine rest for the trip home. We took the Sorrel and Black to the corral and pulled the saddles off. Carl winked at me and said, "Don't tell mother, but when I saw you coming, I brought Ol' Baldy in and gave him a bait of oats, so he would be ready, just in case he was needed."

"Oh, ho, you're so right!" we had a good laugh, as we rubbed down Ol' Baldy and put my saddle on him. Carl was still chuckling when I swung into the saddle and rode though the gate, When I passed the house Betty Sue came onto the porch and waved, "Hurry back, Rob".

When I raised my hand, Ol' Baldy took that as an excuse to run. He was fresh and needed exercise, so I let him set his own pace. We were down the lane and on the road to town before he decided to slow down for a breather.

For the first hour, I couldn't get my mind off Betty Sue. I just couldn't believe she had said "yes" to being my girl. I was always so shy around girls, Most of the guys in my school and Church didn't seem to have that problem. Anyway I couldn't figure out how a pretty girl like her could be interested in a big lug like me. I had never seen her flirt with the boys like some of the girls did, so I couldn't believe that she would invite me to come and see her if she didn't mean it.

About half way to town, the lack of sleep began to catch up with me and I began to doze in the saddle. I must have slept or dozed more than a hour, we had just crossed a sand wash, and headed up the grade toward the old trading post, just out side of town, when two riders came out of nowhere, and pulled their horses up on both sides of me. "So you're the guy that shot Noland's arm off."

They must have been friends of Noland, for they sure weren't very friendly to me.

I had been dozing so I had both hands on the top of the saddle horn to prop myself up. I needed time to get fully awake so I began to bluff, "Did he get to town without bleeding to death".

"No thanks to you."

"You know he was stealing cattle and resisting arrest."

"Why you .., country......". He had a gun pointed at me, but raised it and took a swing at my head with it. I ducked, hoping that Ol' Baldy knew the same roping signals that we used. Pulling on the reins I shoved one stirrup forward and the other heel in his ribs. He sat back on is haunches and whirled around. It worked! He knocked both riders off balance. I pulled my gun and kept backing Baldy up. The horse we backed into, didn't get out of the way soon enough for him, so he laid his ears back and reached around to bite the horse, missed it and bit the rider on the leg just above the knee.

The rider was wearing big Mexican spurs, which indicated that he had little thought for his horse, and was probably a bar-room cowboy, that we called a loafer, who were always looking for a job, but never worked long at any. Well when he jumped from the horse bite he jabbed one of those spurs deep in his horse's flank. His horse got out of the way alright. He jumped straight up in the air and came down hard on his front legs, and never stopped jumping. I was sure that no bar-room cowboy was going to stay on long, so I shoved my gun back in the holster and jumped my horse right into the flank of the other horse, at the same time slapped him as hard as I could with my reins, and he stampeded up the road toward town, with the bit in his mouth, his rider was yelling and yanking on the reins to no avail.

I used the opportunity to ride on up toward the trading post on the top of the hill. Ol' Baldy was not a bit excited, He just acted like it was all in a days work, and not nearly as tough as roping a big steer, or old cow that's trying to protect her calf.

I kept my eyes open for the run away rider. Sooner or later, his horse would tire and he could gain control again, but I didn't think his type would do anything without a helper or two. When I stopped at a little stream that always ran cool with mountain water, to let my horse drink, I looked up at the sun which looked like it was just right above the Mountains. We hadn't made very good time while I was sleeping, and I would have to hurry if I got back to the Boucher's before it was late.

When I stepped into the sheriff's office he was just filling his cup from the pot on the stove. He didn't even look up. "Coffee?"

"Yeah, I think I will, I went to sleep on the way to town."

"Um-ha, a guy don't get enough rest sleeping out on the ground like you have lately."

"I must have been sound asleep when those two guys jumped me in that little ravine just beyond the trading post."

The sheriff whirled around in his chair so fast he spilled hot coffee on his knee. "What happened?"

"Oh, just a couple of loafers rode up looking for the guy that shot Noland in the arm." The look that the sheriff gave me over the rim of his cup was full of questions, so I continued. "If they had spent more time on a horse instead of a stool, their horses wouldn't have gotten the best of them."

Setting his cup down, and raising an eyebrow, he gave me the opportunity to change the subject, so I told him about finding Old John's body.

"Now I wonder which one of those hombres did that?"

The sheriff leaned back, scratched his head, and smoothed out his hair.

Well, Sheriff, the way I see it, only three of those boys are mean enough to do a thing like that, and Noland was with the cattle. That leaves either Jack or Ross, and Jack was watching Pa. So when Pa got away, Jack would have headed for our place looking for him. He must have come upon old John, and killed him.

"Boy, you have a way of butting into my business."

"I stood up and raised my hands over my head, and mocked, "Shoot low Sheriff, I'm crawlin'. " The sheriff stood up when I dropped my arms and with a lopsided grin tapped me on the shoulder and said, "You're okay Kid, in a couple more years I think I might just trade jobs with you."

Now it was my turn, "That might be okay for me, Sheriff, but it takes a young man to work cattle."

We both knew he was joking, but he used his, I'm the Sheriff voice, "You get out of my town, and I don't want to see you back here until the trial"! Oh by the way, tell everyone out there for me that the territorial Judge is coming though a week from Thursday. Bring in Missouri for me."

"Oh I forgot to tell you Sheriff, he has a job working for Drenon at the Crow's Nest."

"Good, how did he do on the drive?"

"Fine, he knows cows and he is a good worker."

The sheriff nodded and reached for the coffee pot. "More Coffee?'

"No I think I'll get back to ranching."

He set the pot back down, "Hold up a minute, I want to ride out past the trading post with you."

"No need Sheriff, I can handle a couple of loafers."

"I know, but I don't want to have to throw you in jail for shooting someone in my town."

The sheriff's horse was at the hitching rail. True to form, He asked several questions while we rode. At the trading post, we said goodbye and I turned Ol' Baldy loose and let him run a little to warm up for the long ride. Halfway up the next rise, I looked back, and the sheriff was still waiting for me to ride out of sight.

I kept my eyes open on the way home, but it turned out to be a long lonely ride. I believe Ol' Baldy was aware that I was in a hurry to get him home before dark, for he stepped right out. He was a good horse with stamina to work all day. When we hit the lane turning into the Boucher's ranch, he was less tired than I, for he broke into a run. I was too tired to want to hold him back. He knew what he could take better than I. We just loped right up to the water tank and stopped.

I used the momentum of the stop to help me out of the saddle. It is a simple trick I learned when I first became a daring teenager. You just let yourself fall to the left while the right leg comes up over the back of the horse, then as the leg starts down you pull yourself up with the right hand and the saddle horn, and land on your feet running. This time when Ol' Baldy felt me falling he just naturally stepped to the right, making room for me right beside the water tank. I ducked down under the hitching rail, and wrapped a line around it. I must have surprised Ol' Baldy for he just looked at me wide eyed and blew a snort.

Mrs. Boucher and Betty Sue served up a hot dish of stew that they had warmed over. As I sat down Mrs. Boucher sat down across the table and Betty Sue just around the table corner from me and folded her hands, I knew I was expected to ask a blessing. I had been praying out loud all my life so it was no problem to thank the Lord for His protection and for family, good friends and the food.

While I ate, Betty Sue never moved from my elbow. I was a little surprised to see her let her mother wait on me, but it sure was nice having her close by. She seemed to know how to get me to talk. She asked me all about the trip to town and what the Sheriff said.

I finished up by telling them about the trial, a week from Thursday and ended by bragging on Ol' Baldy, and the way he handled those other horses. "He sure is a smart horse to behave like that with a stranger riding and all."

Carl had just come in, "He is a smart horse. Smart enough to know a good rider too."

I don't handle compliments well, so I just grinned and looked at my empty cup, Which Mrs. Boucher filled right away.

The big clock in the other room struck eight and Betty Sue turned to me and said, "you don't have to go home until morning do you?

When I look up Mrs. Boucher had her back turned, and was busy at the stove, dipping up some hot water. I looked at Carl and he just nodded his head.

"Daddy has a hammock that swings from the porch post. It would be much cooler there than in the bunkhouse, and cleaner too. No one has cleaned the bunkhouse lately."

I stood up and Carl offered to help with the dishes. Betty Sue opened the door to the porch and I followed, not knowing what else to do. It did seem sort of natural.

We sat on the porch for a while, and now that we were alone, I couldn't think of a thing to say.

It wasn't long before Betty Sue stood up, "Let's go for a walk."

As we walked down the lane to the first bend, Betty Sue asked about seeing the wagon tracks in the grass on the bluff.

"Do you believe that we who trust God, have a special help from Him?"

"Yes I do, I believe that it was God that caused me to look at just the right time to see the wheel tracks. They could only be seen from one place in the road."

I took her hand and we walked back past the windmill. I released the lever to turn it on. And taking down the old dipper hanging on the wire hook, I rinsed it out and offered Betty Sue a drink. She drank and handed me the dipper which I filled and downed a couple of dippers full before hanging it back up and turning off the windmill.

As we walked over by the corral fence, I noticed that the gate between the corral and the horse pasture was open. I gave my whistle for Ol' Dan. He arched his neck and kicked up his heels and come running, with the black right beside him.

I was leaning with my arms folded on the top rail of the fence and had to dodge as his head went past mine while he put his head over my shoulder. I reached out and scratched his neck and patted him, telling him he was a good old pal.

The black had come up to Betty Sue for a pat when the big sorrel turned with his head across her neck and pushed her away, coming between us and the black, then he darted back through the gate into the pasture.

"I think he just told you he's not planning on going home after dark," laughed Betty Sue."

I turned to Betty Sue, "I think he has found a girl friend too. So I guess I'll have to stay, if my horse won't go home till morning."

"I guess so," Betty Sue laughed, but turned toward the house.

We walked silently back to the porch I was thinking how nice it was to be near this young lady, better that I ever dreamed.

I noticed that Carl had put up the hammock, which I took as an invitation to stay the night, so Betty Sue and I could get better acquainted. I guessed that her parents were not unhappy to have me sit out with their daughter.

After a while, we began to talk about little things, mostly about how we had trained our horses and how they were given to us.

When the big clock struck ten, Betty Sue stood up and told me good night, then whispered, "I need to go before Daddy calls for me."

Sure enough as I heard Betty Sue go up stairs, I heard the creak of a rocker and Carl called out, "Sleep well son, don't let that hammock throw you, in the night.

"Thank you, I won't."

Now hammocks aren't bad sleeping until you try to turn over. I was so tired that it was early light before I woke enough to turn over. I started to change positions a couple of times, then decided I didn't want to anyway. It was just barely light enough to see the barn, when I decided to go out and round up my horse and get him ready for the ride home. He came when I called him. In short order, I lead him out and tied him to the windmill.

I didn't expect to see Betty Sue this early in the morning. My reasoning was that she had no cause to be up for a couple of hours. I sure wouldn't have been, except that I wanted to get an early start home while it was cool.

Carl was leaning on the porch post as if he had nothing in the world to do. I guess he was waiting for me, so I walked over.

"Sleep well last night?"

"Yes, but I had enough of not being able to turn over, I think hammocks were made for napping. Along toward morning, I felt the need to change positions and couldn't, so I got up. I wanted to get an early start anyway."

"Mother had it figured that way, too. I don't know what got into my women folks, for they never get up this early except for something special."

I looked over at my horse, "Ol' Dan is all rested up and ready to get along home."

"You better stay for breakfast. The women folk got up early to fix it for you. I'd never be able to eat it all by my self."

"I thought if I left now, I could get home about the time Pa finished the chores, and then I could eat breakfast with him."

"No need to ride thee hours on an empty stomach, when you can sit right down with good company and have breakfast before you go."

Carl put a hand on my shoulder and we walked around to the wash stand and got ready for breakfast.

What a breakfast it was too, fresh fried potatoes, eggs, a thin fried steak and a stack of pancakes, just in case there wasn't enough of everything else to fill up on.

Betty Sue sat across the table from me and every time I looked up the happy twinkle in her eyes caused me to smile. There wasn't much conversation, and once I looked out of the corner of my eye at Carl and caught a quick wink at Mrs. Boucher, only to see her raise one eyebrow and smile at him.

For the first time in my life, I felt at ease in the presence of Betty Sue, so as I slid my chair back a couple inches and finished my coffee, I said, "This sure was good ladies, but if I eat any more I'll have to get off and run along side Ol' Dan, to get comfortable again,"

What I liked about Carl, he could say something funny about anything. "I think you should get off and walk any way. With all the riding you have been doing lately you're about to wear out your hip pockets."

We all smiled and when I stood up, everyone stood. I thanked the ladies for the good breakfast, and started for the door with Betty Sue not a half step behind me. She walked alongside and pretended to help me tighten the cinch on the saddle. Once in a while our arms bumped, and most of the time I could feel the sleeve of her blouse rub my arm. I wasn't used to this, but I sure liked having her so close.

With a small jerk of finality, I put the stirrup in place, not wanting the moment to come to an end. I put my left hand on the saddle horn as if to mount. I knew if she took one step toward me I would reach out to her. She stepped back to make room for me to swing up on my horse.

Safely on my horse, I reached out a hand, that she accepted and then she asked, "Shall I fix a picnic basket for Sunday? Mother and Dad are visiting the Johnson's after Church, and I could catch up with them there for a ride home?"

My heart did a flip that made my head spin, "Hey that will be great I'll bring my buggy."

I was fixing up an old buggy, replacing all the worn and rotten wood. All that was left was to stain it to preserve the wood and make it look new. Well it would never look new for the top was worn out, but it had stake pocket for a flat top that I could make out of a piece of canvas, which could be stained red. I could see the rig now. I had already stained the box and frame black. With the wheels yellow with red hubs and red top, it would be the sharpest looking rig in the row on Sunday.

On the way home, I thought on that buggy so much that I could have made it over a dozen times. I had everything I needed but the fringe for the top. I'd ask mother about that, but I didn't think there was enough time before Sunday to make one.

Because of the early start, I arrived home shortly after mid morning. I was weary from all of the excitement of the last week. When I pulled the saddle off my horse he didn't wait to be rubbed down, He just trotted out into the pasture, rolled a couple of times and loped off to graze.

Pa came by about that time and picked up my saddle, leaving me just the bridle to carry, and started for the tack room of the barn, I was right behind him when he hung up the saddle. There hanging on the wall just above easy reach was the end of he broken tongue I had brought home. The plug was loose in the end. Pa saw me looking at it and placed a hand on my shoulder, "Mother said you wanted it saved, so we guessed that you knew what was hidden in the end."

"I though that you might have hidden any left over money from the cattle sale."

"You are right son, there have been so many holdups lately that I drilled that hole and carried the check from the cattle sale in it for safety. It was a good idea too, because I was held up on the way to town but I managed to surprise them and get away."

"Was it the same men that held you up on the way home?"

"I believe so. Even though they wore masks, I could still get a good look at them. There is a lot more to a man than his chin and nose that can identify him."

I jumped up on a barrel turned upside down and looked at the tongue more closely. He had drilled a hole right in the end of the tongue a little larger than a twenty dollar gold piece. The space between the two bolts that held the iron bracket on the end of the tongue was about long enough to hold twenty five to thirty, Twenty dollar gold coins.

"Great idea Dad, no one would dream of looking there for money."

"You know son, I believe God gives us ideas like this when we need them, if we are trusting in Him. The Scriptures say that if in all our ways we acknowledge Him, he will direct our path.

We started toward the house, I always stop to say hi to mother after being gone for some time.

"Say Pa, those guys were after more than money, for the holdups were in some way tied together with the cattle rustling."

"Yes, I'm sure! I can't help but think that some one is behind the whole thing."

We washed up at the back door and I left my dusty hat on a peg, stepped into the kitchen and greeted mom. "What's cooking Ma?"

"you're always hungry, sit down, the coffee's hot and there are some fresh cookies to go with it. Have you had breakfast?"

"Sure, Mrs. Boucher was up and fixed some."

While we had coffee, I asked if we had enough new canvas to make a flat top for my buggy. Pa thought so. We talked about the best way to dye it red. Pa thought that red was a rather loud color. But mother just smiled like she knew something that Pa hadn't thought about. She seemed to know that young men of my age were not interested in buggies, unless they were thinking of taking someone along.

"I say now", Pa wanted to know, "What is all the interest in that buggy all of a sudden?"

Ma smilingly answered, "Oh he's been working on that old buggy for a long time."

"Pa, do you think I could have enough time off to get it finished before Sunday?"

He raised his eyebrows, so I went on. "Betty Sue and I are planning a picnic after Church on Sunday, and I'll need a buggy."

"Well, if you have to have a buggy by Sunday, we had better get started."

I finished my coffee, reached for two more cookies, and started for the tool shed where the unfinished buggy sat covered with dust. I had just begun staining the wheels yellow when Pa came in and began measuring for the top.

He shaped the side rail, notched them for the cross pieces, glued and clamped it all together in about half the time it would had taken me. By the time I had stained the last wheel yellow he had the frame for the top finished and clamped on the work table.

While I uncorked the mineral spirits and cleaned my hands, Pa rolled out a piece of new canvas he had been saving and we measured it and cut it ready for stain. Pa put a foot up on a sawhorse, rested an arm on his knee and watched as I added boiled oil to red paint until I had a very liquid red stain that I brushed on the underside of the canvas top. When I looked up Pa had walked over and was examining the seat. I had already stripped off all the old leather and stained the wooden frame, but had left the bare springs, not sure what to do next. Without a word, Pa walked away. When he returned, he was carrying an arm full of burlap. He shook out two bags that looked almost new, "these should work to hold the springs in place while we cover the seats. Its not as good as leather, but I believe there is enough canvas to make some good looking seat covers."

"Yes, but how are we going to finish it to make it look right?'

"I'll show you how to lacquer them, and so that when they are finished they will look like fake leather."

Pa showed me how to stretch the burlap over the springs and stitch the springs in place. When we had almost finished, he sent me to the house to see if Mother had some quilt batting, for seat cushions.

I had just reached the shop door when he stood up and said, "Take a look, where is the sun?" I looked and answered, "about half past dinner time." He dropped the tools he had been using and remarked,

"It's been a long time since I've gotten so involved that I worked past lunch time. Let's go see if mother saved us anything to eat."

As we ate lunch, we gave mother a detailed progress report. She suggested that we stitch some denim, that she had, to the burlap to protect the quilt batting, and to make it last longer.

When we had relaxed a few minutes after lunch, Pa opened the family Bible and began to read from James I "If any man lack wisdom, let him ask of God that gives to all men liberally." Then he prayed for wisdom to understand seat making so that we could do the right thing as we rebuilt it. He remembered Missouri, his job, and his faith in Christ.

When we were ready to go back to work, Ma suggested we help her with the dishes and she would come out and help sew on the denim. I was never one to get excited about washing dishes, but I could sense that she wanted to be a part of this buggy project.

Pa stood up with a grin, "Rob, since we can't go any farther with those seats without batting, and we don't know where the batting is, I guess we are trapped," He put a arm around Mother and pushed her away from the dish pan, Go get the batting, we will take over here."

The three of us walked back to the work shop together. They walked arm in arm. Pa looked down at ma, "Remember our first few buggy rides?" Ma smiled, "Oh you romantic, you haven't thought of those rides for years."

"No, but watching our son grow up is the next best thing."

She just smiled and slipped an arm through mine, " We like Betty Sue, She is just the kind of girl we would want for you."

I could feel my ears getting red. I had never talked in such a bold manner about girls with my parents before. I was glad when I could show mother what we had done. It was easier to talk about buggies than girls.

Soon we were busy stitching and tacking layers in place. Mother showed us how to stitch it all together so that it would look much like a machine stitch. I noticed that Pa stepped back when the fine stitching started, but I watched closely, and was soon doing much of the stitching myself. While we were stitching, Pa was at the work bench rubbing bees wax into a strong string to anchor the seat buttons on the seats.

The afternoon slipped away as we stitched, stained, tacked and painted. When at last the seat was fastened in place with screws, Pa dug around in his storage closet and came out with a square gallon can. When he set it down, he said, "Son I think there is enough lacquer here to give everything a good coat to seal it against the weather. Make sure that you get two coats on the top and the seat covers.

When Ma started for the house and Pa left to start chores, I stood for a few minutes just looking it over. I hoped Betty Sue would like it. I had to admit it was a good job, and looked almost like a new buggy. Without the extra help, I could never have finished in time, or have gotten the seats to look like new. With all that we had accomplished today, I knew I could finish it first thing tomorrow and the lacquer would have plenty of time to dry before Sunday.

I worked at the chores with excitement and a strange feeling. I felt that Betty Sue was right here with me, and approved of every move that I made.

When the chores were finished and supper over, I made one more trip to the work shop, just to look every thing over again. Sleep was crowded out of my mind that night by picnics, buggy rides and Betty Sue. It was hours before I could calm down to sleep, and when I did, I dreamed of beautiful smiles and yellow buggy wheels.

The next morning, mother came to the work shop, just as I was stretching the canvas over the top frame. From a large sewing bag she took a length of buggy top fringe, made of heavy cotton string, dyed yellow to match the wheels. The top edge looked like it was an eight strand braid and hooked into the side of the braid was a row of balls and bangles, evenly spaced with a fine job of crochet work. That showed quality and great care. "I thought I would surprise you with this little, something special."

"It was just what I wished for, Mother, but I didn't ask for it because I didn't think you would have time to do it."

I looked at it for so long that she asked, "Do you think it is too frilly for your buggy?"

"No Mom, its just what I wanted, but......"

"Good! Then let's see if it is going to be long enough."

She must have measured the top when she was out here yesterday, for it reached all the way around with just a three inch lap.

Chapter 7

When I pulled into the Church yard Sunday morning, my buggy and I made quite a show. I talked pa into letting me use his high stepping matching buggy team.

Bonnets turned to look, men and boys were crowded around by the time I pulled up to the rail. My friend Sam, tied the horses to the rail and came around to my side as I stepped down,

"Is this the one you were working on? It looks different than the last time I saw it."

"Same one, What do you think?"

He had a way of smacking his lips, with a roll of his tongue. "Looks better than new. "Who's the girl?"

"Who said anything about a girl?"

"Oh, I just never saw you with a fancy buggy before."

Everyone laughed, and there were a few more remarks that I didn't want to answer, so I just stood back and let them know that it was a family project, "Oh we sort of work together at out house."

The men nodded and the boys just rubbed a hand over the smooth wood and looked up at the fringed top.

Having given proper honor for the work well done, the men moved toward the Church. Just Sam and I were left standing by the buggy, and he had just put a hand on my shoulder and was propelling me toward the Church, when the Bouchers drove in with their two seated buggy with the top up.

Betty Sue hopped down and ran over, "Hi Rob, Sam, who's buggy?"

Sam nodded at me, with what looked like half a smirk and half grin.

"Oh Rob! It's beautiful!"

Sam who always acted as if he knew what was going on, just shrugged his shoulders and swaggered to the Church, Leaving the two of us to walk together. I couldn't help but straighten my shoulders when I felt Betty Sue's hand on my arm as we walked up the steps. I'm afraid I missed most of the sermon, for this was the first time I had sat with a girl in Church. All the little girls kept looking at us and smiling; and the young people our age acted like we weren't even there, or that we should be ignored for sitting together.

No one said a word as we passed out of the Church. Betty Sue retrieved the basket from under the seat of their buggy, We backed away from the rail and drove off, while everyone but the children gave us no notice.

We started out in the direction toward where Betty Sue would meet her parents, then after a few miles, we turned off on a seldom used trail that led out into the prairie.

We didn't have much to say, but we smiled a lot at each other. Just being together was enough. There was no need for conversation.

Soon we came to a grassy spot that supported very little cactus. I pulled the buggy around so that it would give us a little shade and tied the team to a weight that I had carried under the seat. While Betty Sue spread a blanket and set out the lunch, I brought a jug of water from the back of the buggy.

What a picnic! Fried chicken, potato salad, baked carrots, and six halves of deviled eggs, baked pinto beans and apple pie. I reached across the food and took Betty Sue's hands and ask God's blessing. "Lord bless our friendship and time together and also the food that Betty Sue has put so much work into getting it ready,"

Betty Sue handed me a plate and when I began to fill it she asked, "Rob, have you pieced together this whole thing about the holdup, kidnapping and rustling?"

"Well, it all seems to fit together, but I haven't figured out why."

"Me either, Dad thinks someone in town is behind it, but it doesn't make sense to me."

"At first I began to wonder if it was a neighbor that wanted to expand his range, but the only one I can think of, that I don't trust, has a ranch between us and his range."

We talked freely of the things we had heard and what we thought about them. It was easy to share our feelings and thoughts without embarrassment, I think I was surprised to find that I could be with a girl and not feel shy.

Eating out of doors always makes me hungry, so I did a man size job of showing Betty Sue that she was a good cook. When I was filled up, I told her she was just about the best cook in the country,

For an answer she smiled and reached into the basket and pulled out a lemon, holding it up, with an, "I did this for you, look". "I had daddy bring it from town just for us."

Her smile was so full of sparkle, that for the first time today I felt my ears turn red.

She produced a metal container, rinsed off the lemon and cut it into small pieces, and added water. Then taking a small paper package from the basket, she unfolded it and dumped the contents into the lemonade, looking up at me with a happy smirk, said, "Sugar".

It was pleasant just to watch her be so happy, I just sat there and waited, Soon she filled my tin cup with lemonade and passed it to me. I suppose her anxious look was because I was so quiet, but when I smiled and said, "Thank you," she tried the lemonade and said, "It would be better if the water was cooler."

"If I'd had this last week, I could have put some ice in it."

"Maybe you could, but you'd not get me out for a picnic in a hail storm, Robert McCloud."

"Oh, are you better than us poor cowboys, who ride I rain and hail, dust and heat?"

"Rob, you're hopeless. I think I'll just begin to pick up the lunch and walk home."

"Oh don't do that, I like your company," I laughed, "you wouldn't want the neighbors to think we fought on our first date."

She looked up at me under her eye lashes, "second date, do you think I didn't plan for you to ride home with me the other day". With this she got up on her knees and began to pick up the leftovers and store them carefully in the basket.

"Oh that was your idea was it." I couldn't frown for laughing. I leaned over and offered to help her, but she put a hand on my arm and said, "Get the horses ready, this won't take but a minute."

By the time the horses were untied and the weight placed in the buggy, she was waiting for me to help her into the buggy.

This was something new. Until today she had never needed any help. Many times I had seen her bounce up into her father's buggy after Church on Sundays.

The team responded to a light tug on the reins and stepped over, so that there was more room between the front wheel and the step. She took my arm, stepped lightly up into the buggy, and slid over to make room for me, but when I stepped up and sat down, I noticed that I had to squeeze in between the side of the seat and my rider.

The team moved out as soon as I tightened the reins.

"That was a wonderful picnic lunch," I felt her hand come up under and around my arm, "Thank You, I loved planning it for you."

"Us!" I smiled.

"Us", she had the sweetest laugh.

As we rode along I kept thinking. What can we do for an excuse to go riding again? We sure couldn't go on a picnic every week, Then I spoke out loud the thought that come to my mind, "Do you think your folks would let you ride with me to the court trials next week?"

"Oh, I hope you are going to ask me first?"

I knew she was teasing, but girls always had a way of making me make dumb blunders when they talked to me like that. I started to get embarrassed, then caught myself before I said anything.

Ma'am, I would be pleased to have your company, on the ride to town next week."

She tried to hold a sober face but failed, "Why, thank you Sir, I would be delighted." Then on a lighter note, "But you'll have to ask my father, first,"

Now what did she say that for? It would be much easier for her to ask him than me. Then I realized that she was telling me that, if I was planning on courting, I had better take it seriously, because she wasn't planning on playing games.

"Ok, if you wish, I'll be glad to."

We took the back trail and our own sweet time getting to our destination. We were both happy, and when we talked it was just small talk. Once in a while, we would share ideas of things we liked, or didn't like, learning a little more about each other.

When we got to the ranch where the Bouchers were having lunch with the Johnson's, we were invited in for a snack before everyone was to go home.

I went along with the men to hitch up Carl's team, and at no time was I able to get him alone so I could talk to him. Finally, when they were all loaded and about to leave, I stepped up to the buggy and looked right at Mr. Boucher and asked, "Would it be all right if Betty Sue rode into town with me next Thursday."

Carl looked over at Mrs. Boucher, and then nodded, "I guess so, if she wants to. Oh, by the way Rob, tell your folks they can come over and ride with us in our two seater."

I touched my hat and stepped back looking at Betty Sue. I knew she felt embarrassed for me by the look of sympathy on her face.

"Bye Rob, see you Thursday."

I don't remember saying good-by to anyone else, for I was half way home before I realized that I was driving the team much too hard for the distance we had to travel.

This whole thing of having a special girl friend with a promise was all new to me and I didn't know for sure what was next, but I liked the feeling I was having at the time.

Chapter 8

P a had made arrangements with an old cowhand, to do our chores. He had said he had no desire to go to the trial, for he'd seen all he wanted to see of the inside of a court room, On Wednesday night, old Bill come over and stayed in the bunk house. He would stay and see to the chores until we came back, just in case it took more time than a day for the hearing.

Thursday morning, by the light of the lantern, we hitched the buggy team to my red topped buggy, Pa and ma would ride in the seat, so I arranged part of a bag of oats in the box back of the seat and made a place to ride, with my heals hooked in the springs and leaning across the bag of oats, I was almost comfortable. After about an hour, I dozed off to sleep and didn't wake up until we were on the ridge above the Bouchers. When I looked ahead, Ma was sleeping with her head on Pa's shoulder, Pa felt me moving around trying to find a comfortable position, pulled out his watch and looked at the time, The silver case reflected the early morning light. When he snapped the case shut, I thought, "It's a good thing he wasn't carrying it when he was held up".

We made fair time, it's only six thirty. We will have time to give the horses a break at the Bouchers before we go on."

"I don't know about the horses, but I sure need a break. I don't fit back here like I used to."

"If you want to, you can get out and walk, We can pick you up after we water the horses at the Bouchers."

I smiled at his joking, "No thanks, I'll wait."

When we pulled up at the Bouchers windmill, I watered the horses while Ma and Pa went over and greeted them at the front porch. Before I had finished, Betty Sue came over to the buggy with a basket in one hand and a large mug of coffee in the other.

"I packed us a snack for later. Here's some coffee for now."

"Girl, you think of everything! Thank you. Just for that", I teased, "I'll let you ride with me."

"W'y, thank you sir", she chided. Placing the lunch under the seat and stood by as I tied the horses, so they could relax a few minutes.

"You young people had better come and eat while the biscuits are warm," Betty Sue's mother called from the porch. Our parents were sitting around a small table on the porch, drinking coffee and eating biscuits with jelly. Betty Sue bounced up the steps and poured two cups of coffee, she took the plate in one hand and coffee in the other, sat down on the steps, and motioned for me to sit down beside the plate.

I thought "What a girl, I think maybe this is love."

It had been three hours and a half since my light breakfast. I had never given it much thought before, but now I believed that hot biscuits and coffee tasted good to me any time.

With in a half hour, both rigs were on the road. We young people had started first and had a faster team, so before long we were out ahead by almost a mile, It was some feeling to be alone with this special girl, although we were never really alone, for there were a lot of rigs on the road, Sometimes we passed a slow wagon or buckboard. One time we had let our horses walk to give them a breather, a group of young guys passed us riding prancing horses and shouted a few remarks, then as they pulled away, one of them started to da, da ta da, to the wedding march, It made me feel disgusted, then I felt Betty Sue's hand on my arm, and she said, ""Some day they will grow up! Maybe?"

We both laughed and I asked, "Were we ever silly like that?" Then with a stern confidence in her voice, "you were."

"And just how do you know that?"

She just raised an eyebrow and looked out of the corner of her eye.

"I didn't think you noticed."

"You'd be surprised what we girls notice."

I reached up and pulled my hat down over one eye next to her, and then slapping the reins, I clicked to the horses.

As they moved out, Betty Sue took hold of my arm with one hand and laid her head on my shoulder, "you were never as silly as some of the guys."

I was afraid to move. If I was dreaming, I didn't want to wake up. The special moment was over much before I wanted. Before long she was laughing at prairie dogs and streaked gophers, along the road. This was going to be some girl to get to know, one minute very emotional and the next talking or laughing about something else.

As we neared town, I began to wonder about the ruffians that had tried to get me the last time I was in town, I doubted if they would try anything with all the people on the road.

As we came down the slope of the last valley just before the trading post, I saw the young riders that had passed us with all the hoorays, pull out on both sides of the trail and wait for us. As we came up to them I noticed for the first time that all were wearing guns, Then Missouri rode up along side the buggy, with a serious look on his face and said, "We didn't think you should ride into town without an escort."

"Okay, shoot your self."

"I might, but not until I get a shot at anyone that wants to make trouble."

Even though some of these fellows were one or two years younger, I knew they were letting us know that we were all in the battle as neighbors and friends, and they had decided that there wouldn't be any trouble, while Betty Sue was along.

As they split up with some ahead and some behind our buggy, I whispered to Betty Sue, "I think they are growing up faster that we thought," She just nodded.

When we had passed the trading post, Missouri rode up beside us, "Half of us are going to circle back and ride in with your folks, and I'm going on in with you to check in with the sheriff."

The only excitement we had as we came into town was the playful capers of our escort. We headed right for the livery-stable for I was sure we would be here more than one day.

We unhitched and put the horses away, Betty Sue waited by the buggy, I knew that she was handy with horses as I was, but I was sure glad she acted like a lady while the guys were around. I could see that she knew, and would not let me down.

Missouri left with a remark about looking up the Sheriff, and the other guys put away their horses and disappeared from sight, but I knew that they would not be far away at any time.

I washed my hands at the well and walked back to Betty Sue, who was waiting with a smile. We crossed the alley and passed Widow Miller's house on the way to Main Street. She was in the yard when we came by, so not knowing what else to say I asked about the rooms that I knew Pa had already reserved.

"Robby, my boy, you didn't run off and get married did you?"

My face turned all shades of red and my ears burned. "Our folks are coming right behind us. We'll wait for them."

Betty Sue looked sharply at me with a stunned look and Widow Miller, laughed with a big, "Haw, haw."

"Robby, my boy, I thought I'd embarrass you, but you got the best of me on that one."

"Ma'am, you know Betty Sue Boucher?"

"Well I guess I should, as many times as she has stayed with me over the years." She turned to Betty Sue, "you'd better watch this one. He's almost full grown."

Betty Sue gave her one of her big smiles and replied, "Oh I will! I sure will." She reached over and hugged my arm.

Widow Miller grunted, "You two better run along and enjoy yourselves. I have a lot of work to do before company comes. She always called her paying guest, company.

I turned to Betty Sue, "let's go see if the restaurant has some Ice cream,"

While we were waiting for our ice cream, Missouri came up to us, "Rob. The sheriff said he wanted you to come in and see him right away."

"Okay, as soon as we get our Ice cream."

"I'll be glad to take your place and eat ice cream with Betty Sue."

"Maybe you should take my place and go see the sheriff for me."

"I don't think that would work."

"Well if I have to see the sheriff for myself, I'll eat my own ice cream."

"I was just trying to be helpful," He tipped his hat at Betty Sue, and left.

Betty Sue looked at me and her laugh was almost a giggle. We finished our ice cream, communicating mostly with smiles.

The sheriff was waiting in his office when we crossed the street. "To keep you out of trouble with that gun, that I know you don't want to give up, I'm going to make you my deputy while you are in town."

"Thanks anyway Sheriff, but I've brought Betty Sue with me as my guest."

"Her folks are coming in aren't they?"

"Yes, but….."

"I'm going to need you, Rob, I've seen how you use that gun, and you're not kill happy like some of these would-be gunmen."

"Sheriff, I appreciate you confidence, but I'm here to show Betty Sue a good time."

"You see Rob, we still don't know who hired those thieves, and the way I figure it, you could still be in danger for helping me catch them. I don't think any of these young fellows that he is hiring, will take a chance with a star on your chest. They know they could never get away, and the penalty for shooting a law officer is too high a price to pay for someone of their experience."

I just stood there and looked at him. All of a sudden I didn't want to be grown up, for it meant giving up something I wanted to do. Today I had my plans all made, and I was planning on just walking around town with Betty Sue, knowing people were watching us. I wanted every one to know that Betty Sue was my girl. My plans did not include letting her sit with her parents while I played deputy. I was just about to say no, when Betty Sue stepped to my side so she could look right into my face, "It's Okay, Rob, I'll be all right. I think you owe it to your Pa, to help out right now.

I looked at her for a moment before I answered, "All right Sheriff, if you think it will help."

"Good! I was hoping I could count on you. Now raise your right hand, and repeat after me."

When we were finished with the swearing in, he pinned a star on my shirt pocket. It felt heavy and make my shirt sag. Every move I make, it reminded me that it was there. I wasn't sure I liked it.

"You two run along now, and see the sights; I'll meet you at the court house just before the trial starts. And stay out of trouble."

We stepped into the street, hand in hand. I had the feeling that this new job was going to interfere with our good time. I was sort of disappointed, yet elated about being picked as a deputy. We walked down the street looking in windows. It wasn't until the third window that I realized that I was still holding Betty Sue's hand. I hadn't seen a thing in the windows. I squeezed her hand and she smiled, but never offered to remove it. We had passed everything from shoes to hats, to jewelry, although we didn't stop at the jewelry window. I guess that Betty Sue didn't want me to get any idea that we were ready for that just yet.

We had just come to the corner and turned to cross main street when the three trouble makers who had bothered me the last time I was in town, came up from behind us.

"Well, lookie here", one twanged. "If it isn't Sonny Boy and he has a girly with him too."

I turned my back on him and started across the street, when he grabbed my shoulder and spun me around.

"No body turns his back on me." He bellowed. Then he saw the badge, "Oh and he's even wearing a toy badge." He sneered, "Does your mommy know you're out alone?" His first finger of his left hand came up under the badge and I thought it would rip off my shirt pocket.

The look on his face changed, "Hey fellows. I believe it's real. Where'd you find one like that, Sonny Boy?" He reached for the badge, "I'll just take that, someone might mistake you for a deputy, and get you into trouble."

My left hand came up over the badge. At the same time, Betty Sue let go of my right hand, and it stopped on my gun.

"I got this from the sheriff and with it the authority to make arrests for assaulting an officer and disorderly conduct."

They all stepped back, with their hands slightly above their elbows, so I relaxed just a little, and continued, "Now I don't think you guys want to miss the trial, so don't let me see you again until it's over."

I turned my back again and placed my right hand on Betty Sue's back, started across the street. There weren't enough people around for our little caper to attract attention, and I wanted to get Betty Sue back where there was a crowd, just in case someone started something.

We used up the morning, with our heads in the clouds, and in our own little world. It had almost gotten us into trouble. I now felt a little disappointed and confused. I knew that there was trouble brewing, and needed to stay alert, but I wanted to give my whole attention to Betty Sue today, and not be bothered with anything else.

By the time we walked back to the restaurant, it was full; and the owner had set up picnic tables and tables made of planks on saw horses with benches made of planks on nail kegs.

While we looked for a place to sit, Pa walked up and put a hand on my shoulder, "I see the Sheriff found you."

When I turned, there was Ma, Pa and the Bouchers. Carl moved over beside Betty Sue and said with a smile, "I see you have a very important man with you today."

"I think so, but he is an important man any day," she smiled at her father's raised eyebrows, with a smile that said, don't tease me in public, or else! Then she continued with, "You should have seen him handle those trouble makers."

Just then, Mrs. Boucher spotted a table just the right size for six. We hurried over to it just in time, for others were moving in the same direction, As we seated the ladies, Carl looked over the crowd and remarked, "I believe the whole country came to town today, I think the sheriff should sell tickets to the court. He could raise his annual salary in one day. Then he wouldn't have to fine us for spitting on the sidewalk."

"Oh Carl you don't chew and spit on the side walk", Mrs. Boucher pulled at the side of his shirt, "sit down and order us some lunch." He responded by sitting down so fast that he almost tipped over the nail keg bench.

"What's this about trouble makers?" Pa had a frown on his face.

"Oh, just the same guys that tried to cause trouble the last time I was in town." He waited, so I shortened the story as much as possible.

"Did you run into any trouble this morning?" I asked.

"No, the ladies stopped at Widow Miller's to freshen up, and Carl and I spent our time with the state attorney, then we met you here."

As slow as we were getting served, I thought we would be late for court and the sheriff wouldn't like it if I was late meeting him. Finally, a lady brought our food. With this crowd there was little choice. She just brought plates of food and collected for it while she was there.

Then I saw the sheriff coming though the crowd, with a plate full of food, to my surprise he came right up to the end of our table and sat down, pushing back things to make room for his plate.

"Sorry to intrude folks, but I need to talk to my deputy."

He began eating, and a waitress brought him a cup of coffee and refilled ours.

"Rob, when we are through with lunch, I want you to go back with me. You sit with me on the right side of the court room where we can see what's going on in the crowd." He took a few more bites, "Your folks can come later, there will be a place reserved for them, they're witnesses."

Carl looked up, "You selling tickets for this shindig, Will?"

"Now Carl, why didn't you think of that sooner, that's just about the best idea I've heard all day." Everyone laughed. The sheriff pushed back his plate and finished his coffee. Then standing up, "Well come on Rob, we have work to do."

As we moved through the crowd toward the sheriff's office, the sheriff explained to me what he had planned. "Rob, I am sure there is someone behind this whole thing and before this trial is over I want him in jail."

I nodded, "Do you have anyone in mind?"

"We don't have much to go on. More than one person that I talked to has lied to me, but I need more than that."

"Do you have any suspects?"

"Well, not good ones, but I sure hope this trial will reveal who is behind this mess."

As we walked up to the sheriff's office he turned to me with a very serious look on his face, "Rob, the reason I made you a deputy for the day, is because of the way you handle a gun, without wanting to shoot up any one, So don't let me down. Keep your head, and don't pull that gun unless it is absolutely necessary."

I nodded as we entered the office. He proceeded to give the regular deputies instructions for moving the prisoners to the court room, and where every one was to stand guard during the trial. When he was sure that everyone understood their duties, he tipped his hat, rubbed the top of his right ear, and with half a smile said, "On days like this I wish the city council would hurry up with their proposal to make an addition to the court house to annex the jail."

When I thought on this, I came to a full realization of why we needed extra deputies. Someone out there would not want the prisoners to talk. Moving them might be dangerous for any one of them, if they knew the boss.

"All right, let's get started." The first two deputies moved out to watch the alley while others brought out the prisoners. The sheriff motioned for me to follow on the left side while he took the right side. We entered the court house without an incident.

The court room was filled to overflowing when we entered. As we took our places, the sheriff whispered, "Look the crowd over good. Be sure you know where everyone is, and look for anything out of order."

I was still looking while the judge was seated and order was called. I missed most of the presentations of the attorneys, but when the witnesses were called, Pa was the first one on the stand, telling his story.

Next Missouri gave his story, again denying knowing who was behind all the these events, When the prisoners were questioned they all tried to deny any knowledge of the rustling or holdup, It appeared to me that there was an attempt to make it look as if the two events were not connected.

The prosecution asked every witness the same question, "Who is behind these events, and who hired you?" Everyone denied any knowledge. Finally by the end of the long afternoon, there was no new evidence. The Judge recessed until nine o'clock tomorrow morning.

The sheriff signaled me into position with a nod, while he took his place on his side, ready to move out just ahead of the prisoners.

The light of the late evening was fading fast. I could see well enough to assure myself that the alley and street at the end were clear. Just as Noland stepped out the door, something made a slight move on the roof of the store building across the street. At first glance I could tell it was no bird. I drew and fired a rifle barrel bounced up. I fired again, pieces of brick and mortar splattered, and someone on the roof swore.

"Inside", shouted the sheriff, as he motioned with his gun toward the side door of the jail. The deputies hurried the prisoners into the jail. I followed the sheriff to the back of the store building, moving back about twenty feet, where we could see up the slopping roof. On the roof sat a man rubbing his eyes as he crouched undercover of the false sides of the building.

"Game's over," commanded the sheriff, "Drop you gun over the side and keep your hands in the air."

A crowd started to gather, and the sheriff said to me, "Rob, keep the crowd back, Carl, bring a ladder from the store room," The ladder was set up to the building and held by Carl and Pa.

"Come down the ladder carefully, don't try anything funny!" The sheriff had things under control. The captive demonstrated a calm attitude and came down without resistance. With all the guns pointed right at him, he had no choice. It was a lucky shot that knocked brick just in his eyes. He was handcuffed and locked in a cell by himself.

I was in a hurry to join Betty Sue, but the sheriff acted so strange that I couldn't help but stay and watch him. He sat in his chair, pulled out a drawer and grabbed a handful of papers, which turned out to be wanted posters. When he grunted, I stepped up and looked over his shoulder. There in front of him, was a picture of the man we took from the roof. "I thought there was something strange about this guy. He's a hired gun, with a price on his head."

"Rob, it looks like you are in the big time. This one has a price on his head. Your quick action saved the life of one of our prisoners. I'll bet he could tell us who is behind all this, but I don't suppose he will."

I'd had enough lawman life for one day, when I looked at Pa and Carl; they both smiled knowingly, and Pa said, "Let's join the ladies for supper at Widow Miller's.

Betty Sue and I sat at a table in our own little world, until Carl and Pa, shared in telling the story of the capture of the famous hired gun. I just sat there half embarrassed; I knew my ears were getting red.

"Rob", asked Widow Miller, "How much is the reward?"

"I don't know, I didn't think to ask."

Carl had a twinkle in his eyes, "He was too interested in- — — getting something to eat."

Betty Sue read her fathers teasing, and covered her grin with her napkin. With a half grin, I filled my fork with mashed potatoes and continued eating.

By the time we had finished eating, it was dark, Betty Sue and I moved toward the door, when Pa stopped us with, "I don't think this would be a good night to go for a walk, there is too much going on, with all the excitement in town."

I could tell by the look on Carl's face that he agreed, and didn't want Betty Sue exposed to what he knew would be going on downtown.

"We'll just sit on the porch a little while."

Carl nodded and my mother smiled. It gave me a good feeling to know that our parents were in favor of our friendship.

When we sat on the porch swing, Betty Sue leaned against my shoulder, placed her hand on my arm and smiled up at me. We didn't need to say a word; I knew what she was saying.

Once again, I was reminded how easy it was to be with her. Neither of us felt it necessary to say a thing. This seemed to be the pattern of our time together, finally she asked, "Will you be helping the sheriff tomorrow?"

"I think so, I sure never dreamed that he would want me to help him. When I first met him he acted like he didn't like me. He must have changed his mind."

"He knows a good man when he sees one."

She stood up with her hand in mine, pulling me to my feet, I knew she was saying that she thought that we needed a good night's rest in order to make the most of tomorrow, The more I saw of this girl, the more I became aware of how sensible she was.

We found our parents in the living room enjoying a good visit. As we entered, the ladies stood up and Mrs. Boucher said, "You men had better not stay up too late."

"Ok, Mother," answered Carl, with a sober look.

I was aware of the arrangements. Because of the crowd in town and the shortage of rooms, the ladies would share one room and the men another, I sat back in a rocking chair and listened to Carl and Pa discuss the trial. Both of them thought that tomorrow one of the prisoners would surely be pressured into telling the name of the leader of the crimes.

After a few minutes, both men stood, Carl looked over to include me, ""Well son, It's been a long day."

We retired to the same room that I had slept in when all this excitement started for me. I lay awake living the weeks over again, trying to analyze all the events to see if I could try to discover why all this had happened. Finally I fell asleep.

When I woke the next morning, Pa and Carl were already up and outside and I could smell fresh coffee. I dressed as fast as possible and hurried down to breakfast. Everyone else was waiting at the table. As I pulled up a chair and sat down. Widow Miller entered with a large tray of Pancakes. Setting them on the table, she stopped at my chair, "Robby, would you like some coffee?"

"Yes, thank you."

After breakfast, Betty Sue and I walked down to the sheriff's office together. As we neared the office, Betty Sue turned to me and said, "Rob, I'm proud of you."

"Thank You."

The sheriff smiled when we came in, "I'm sorry to spoil your holiday kids. Rob, are you ready for another day as the sheriff's right hand man?" Then he looked out the window, reached up and rubbing the top of his ear, and looked at me. "You know Rob. I've been studying you. Your folks have done a good job raising you. There are not many young men I could trust with a job like this."

"Thank you, Sheriff. We have great parents, but one of the things that makes a difference is that they have taught us to believe in the Lord, and live to please Him with our lives. Sheriff, one thing I have learned, is that we cannot live up to God's standards without the power of God in us."

"Well it must be something. Maybe, when this is over, I'll have time to hear about how you get this help from God."

Pa and Carl stopped by, so Betty Sue could go with them to find a place in the court room.

We moved the prisoners without incident, and took the same positions as the day before. The only difference was that today I knew what to do.

Before the Judge came in, the prosecution attorney come over, and asked my age, He informed me that today I would be called on to give a short version of my part as I saw it. Then when he started to walk away, he turned back and said, "The defense attorney will try to trip you up so that your testimony will be thrown out. Don't worry just stick to the truth."

I nodded understandingly. The nervous feeling had not left me, when I was called to the stand. As I walked up, I was wishing that I could be second to testify instead of first.

The sea of faces looked a little blurred. So I quickly asked God to help me say the right things. Just then I heard the attorney for the state ask, "Tell us what you know about this case?"

I started from the beginning, and told the story, just as I have told you, leaving out the part with Betty Sue. It was easy after I got started, an when everyone laughed at the part of Missouri on the prairie with his feet tied to the horse's halter, that cause me to sort of get into the story all the more. When I had finished, the defense attorney stood up with a smirk on his face and said, "You're pretty good with a gun, aren't you?"

"Fair. My Grandfather taught me how to shoot."

"Good enough to capture a gunman, an outlaw, single handed.

"No sir, I was just doing my duty"

"Yes, I see you are wearing a badge, you're pretty young to be a deputy, aren't you?"

"I guess you'll have to ask the sheriff that, Sir."

"The way you tell your story, you think you are quite a hero"

"Objection," the prosecuting attorney interrupted.

"No further questions."

Then the prosecuting attorney, asked me some questions.

"You say you made two trips to Mr. Black's home to find out if your father had been there. Can you give the exact words of Mr. Black when you found him home?"

"No, but he definitely denied that Pa had been there."

"You say you were there twice?"

"Yes, the first time no one answered the door. The second time he was there, He came to the porch and acted as if Pa had never been there and threatened to foreclose on the ranch."

Pa was called to the stand, and witnessed once again that he had paid the mortgage payment.

In the back of the room someone moved. After a glance, I motioned to the sheriff and he raise his commanding voice, "Hold O. B. Black for questioning! Two deputies at the front door blocked the way of escape.

Prosecution put Mr. Black on the stand, "Why did you tell Rob McCloud that you had not seen his father?"

"I don't know what he thinks he is doing, I thought the McCloud was my friends, I helped them buy that ranch. I don't know why the lad has turned against me. I've never done anything to him."

He continued, "All I'm saying is, that he is quite a story teller, everyone can see that."

"What do you think he would gain, if he is telling a lie?"

"All this hero business must have gone to his head."

"Do you think this young man hates you?"

"I don't know of any reason why."

"Do you know any of these prisoners?"

"No, I don't think so, I have no reason to know them. I don't frequent the hang out of town."

"Have you seen any of them before?"

"No".

I looked over at the prisoners, all of them were looking down, except Noland, and he was staring right at Mr. Black, While O.B. Black acted as if he were offended that someone would think he would have anything to do with these loafers.

I hadn't though much about Mr. Black before, but why had he lied?" O.B. Black could foreclose on a valuable ranch if father hadn't made the payment. Every thing that happened to us would affect the payment on the ranch this year or the next. He had already been paid most of the loan, He had sold us the ranch, and now if we failed a payment he would get it back, I decided to talk this over with the sheriff. I again became conscious of the court room in time to hear the prosecuting attorney ask Noland, "If you were being paid to kill someone, and were caught, would you hang before you revealed the name of the one who paid you?"

For the first time Noland became tense, "I didn't kill anybody."

The hearing continued until noon with no breaks, the prisoners had stuck to their story, but couldn't deny being caught stealing cattle and attempted kidnapping. Then the Judge announced a recess until two o'clock, when he would pass sentence. The trial for murder of Old John would start tomorrow.

There was a stir in the crowd, for many of them had not heard of the murder. We had all agreed to leave out the information about the murder until we could see who might talk, revealing the boss behind these crimes.

When the prisoners were moved to jail, I walked over to the sheriff and said, "I can't believe Mr. Black lied." Just then Pa and the prosecuting attorney came into the office. The sheriff was occupied in thought, then he looked up at Pa, "Bob, when was it you bought that place from Black?"

"About ten years ago."

"Do you remember who lived there before you?"

"I don't remember the name, but didn't he lose the place to Black."

"If I recollect right, there was some complaint about losing a check or sale voucher, and the family moved away without filing a complaint, so nothing was done about it."

The attorney spoke up, "Would there be any records around on what happened back then?"

"No, I wasn't sheriff then and those contract sales were seldom recorded."

The attorney had his head down in thought, all of a sudden he raised his head and squared his shoulders, "Sheriff can I try something?" Let me talk to the Prisoners?"

"I don't think their attorney will like it, so make it short." We all walked down the short hall to the cells to see what he had in mind.

"Do you boys know what we do to you in this state for accessory to murder one?" Where do you think you'll spend what Black has promise to pay, after you are sentenced to hang."

The sheriff chimed in, "We know by the process of elimination which one of you murdered Old John. There will be no problem of pinning it on you Jack."

"If we didn't have proof, do you think we could name you?"

"Well, if wasn't my idea."

"Shut up Jack, they're bluffing."

"Ok, but I'm not going to face charges on this one alone, Black can keep his money for all I care."

"Rob", called the sheriff, "lets you and me go round up the Boss of this here thieve' bunch."

I followed him out the door and down the street toward Black's house. We were near the house when I noticed the up stairs front window open about four inches, it dawned on me that we were now at just the right angle for a good shot from that window. Without thinking I shoved the sheriff with my left hand and drew with the right, just as a bullet from the window plowed the path between us. I fired at the lower left corner of the open window. There was the click of lead hitting metal and a howl from someone inside the house. We ran for the door. Inside, Mrs. Black was chewing on her handkerchief, and managed a muffled "go away."

Upstairs, in the front bedroom sat O.B., Black holding his hand to the side of his bloody head. It must have not been a bad wound, for the rifle in his left hand was pointed our way but was moving in little circles.

The sheriff took command and called, "I wouldn't try that. Black, shot anyway and missed, but my shot didn't, I hit his left hand right between the thumb and trigger finger, knocking the gun to the floor, Black howled again.

The Sheriff walked over to the window and shouted, "Someone go fetch the Doc." Then he turned to Black, "Now O.B let me look at that hand."

He moved over to the corner of the bed and lifted up the quilt, loosened the sheet and tore a piece about a foot square from it.

After sopping the blood from Black's ear, we noticed that the bullet had just cut through the top of the ear making it bleed profusely but with very little damage.

"When it's healed you will look like you were ear marked with the yearlings", chided the sheriff, "Now let me see that hand."

The Doctor came in and finished cleaning and bandaging the wounds.

"If this keeps up", muttered the sheriff, we'll have to build a bigger jail. Bad men are showing up behind ever rock and window."

We came out of the house to a large crowd that had gathered because of the shooting.

"It's all over folks, go on about your business," the sheriff was always in command when there was a crowd around.

O.B. Black looked quite harmless with all the bandages on hand and face.

Still his eyes were filled with disgust and hatred. The only thing I could think of was he must be mad because he got caught.

On the way to the jail, we ignored questions like, "What did he do?" "Is he involved too?" "Sheriff, is he the big boss?"

"You didn't make a mistake this time did you, Sheriff"

In a crowd this size, there are always several who stand in the back to jeer and make fun, or try to make a joke. I was sure glad to get inside the sheriff's office.

The jail was full so a deputy put Black in a corner and sat on the desk to keep an eye on him so he wouldn't try to get away, for we would soon move into the court room.

It was already one thirty, and we hadn't had lunch. In about fifteen minutes we would move the prisoners to court.

Maybe the sheriff wasn't hungry, but I sure was. It had been so long since breakfast that it seemed like yesterday.

"Hi! Rob, is anyone hungry around here?" Betty Sue stepped through the door followed by our mothers, "I brought two sandwiches and milk for each of the two best lawmen in town.

"Bless you girl", grinned the sheriff, "I thought we would have to go hungry all afternoon."

"Oh no", retorted Betty Sue, "With all the extra work you've been doing you'll need to keep your strength up."

"Why thank you, young Lady. Just for that, when today is over I'll give you back you boy friend."

Betty Sue stiffened, but would not let the sheriff best her, "Well I hope so! You sure know how to spoil a girl's date."

The sheriff put a hand to his ear, pushed his hat down over his eyes and proceeded to take a big sandwich in both hands and busy himself with eating.

Betty Sue and I went over to a front window and sat on the window ledge while I ate my lunch. We talked quietly about what had happened and why we thought O.B. would be convicted even if he didn't confess.

I was eating the last sandwich when the sheriff got up and motioned the deputies into action, then turning to me said, Rob, I don't think we'll need you, so finish eating your lunch. You can take your place in the court room when you're through." He looked at Betty Sue, and squinted an eye into a half wink and touched his hat as he turned to go.

The Court was packed when we came in. I ushered Betty Sue over to squeeze in with our parents, then took my place with the sheriff. We would have to stand for the session, for there were no chairs left unfilled.

When Court started a few minutes late because of the extra excitement, O.B. Black had a bandage on each hand and one over his ear. We could tell he was well enough to question, because he was mad as and old sidewinder with his rattles cut off.

The prisoners were questioned again, but the attitude had changed. They each blamed the other and all blamed Mr. Black. He shouted denial to no avail, for the witness was too strong against him. Especially when the attorney brought up the first foreclosure on the ranch that we had bought from him, and the strange disappearance of the former buyers.

The Judge swore out charges against O. B Back for conspiring to commit murder, kidnapping, and cattle theft.

Jack was found guilty of murder, kidnapping and theft. The rest were to be sent to the state prison until sentence could be carried out. This had been one of the biggest events in our county since the early day of claim jumping and range wars.

When court was over, I felt the urge to get as far away from people and town as possible.

Chapter 9

That night, after a good meal as Widow Millers, Betty Sue and I were sitting on the porch, when Betty Sue blurted out, "I hate guns! I wish you could quit carrying one."

I didn't know what to say for a few seconds. I was still wearing the badge and carrying my gun. For some reason, with all the excitement of the last few days, I felt uneasy taking the badge off. Except for shooting small game and an occasional a prairie dog, I hadn't used my gun like this before, and I had the strange feeling of wishing it wouldn't happen again.

"Right now, I wish I could too. I've never had to use one like this before, and hope I never have to again."

"I've heard my dad tell about young punks trying to call out for the purpose of out shooing someone that is good with a gun. I don't want that to happen to you. You're too good with that gun and I don't want you to turn into a gunfighter."

"It has been years since that had happened around here. You know that God can keep things like that from happening if we trust him."

"I know, but look what has happened to your Pa. I still don't like it. I guess all this shooting has made me uneasy."

Right then, I decided that if we were going to have the proper kind of relationship we should start praying together.

"I think it would be a good idea if we would take some time to pray about it."

One thing I like about Betty Sue, she didn't hesitate about the things of the Lord. She took both of my hands in hers and started to pray, "Dear Lord, thank you for the way you care about us. Thank you for a friend like Rob. Lord, the last few weeks have been frightful for us, even though they have brought Rob and me closer together as good friends. I'm still afraid of what Rob might be pushed into. I'm afraid that someone will try to out shoot him, causing him to have to shoot someone just to stay alive. Lord, please keep him from that type of life. May we keep our lives dedicated for your purpose. I ask this in Jesus' name.

I continued, "Thank you Lord for giving us safety, I believe you have guided my hands to keep me from killing anyone. For I have trusted you to make me accurate enough so as not to kill. I'm sorry about the hasty shot at Mr. Black. I was so scared of him shooting again, that I just didn't think. It was a miracle that the bullet went where it did, even though he is bad and tried to kill us. It wasn't my place to pass judgment. Thank you again, for protecting me. Thank you for a friend like Betty Sue, for her thoughtfulness and concern. Guide our lives and time together so that in all things we will please you our Lord. We ask these things so that we may give you glory in everything, Amen.

Betty sue leaned her head on my shoulder, and I laid my head on hers. After a moment, she leaned away and gave me one of the sweetest smiles I had ever seen then stood up, I was still holding her hand, returning her smile, when Pa and Carl returned from their walk, came up to the porch.

Carl spoke first, I'm glad to see that you young folks have begun making prayer a part of your time together, the closer your friendship with God, the better friends you'll be to each other."

"Well. Children, Carl and I have talked it over with our women folk and we plan to leave at first light in the morning. Your mothers have planned a picnic breakfast to eat when we are about an hour and half out of town.

Carl continued, "It's a long drive tomorrow so we'd better turn in early."

When morning came, we men rose early and watered the horses, then fed them a bit of oats while we harnessed up. Then after watering them again, we hitched up and went to the porch to retrieve the luggage and picnic baskets with our breakfast.

The sheriff was waiting by the rigs when we came out. As I helped Betty Sue up, the sheriff came over and shook my hand and turned to Pa, "Get this fellow out of town, before he takes over my job. We just can't have him pushing me around and shooting up our prominent citizens."

I caught a wink at Pa and the half wink from the other eye at Betty Sue.

Then he turned to Pa, "You had better keep him at home. I sure could get used to having him working with me."

Then shaking my hand again, with the other hand on my shoulder, "Son, I want to thank you for all your help.

Some day I want to know why you are so much different from these young loafers around town."

"Sheriff," Betty Sue leaned over toward us. "The difference is faith in Christ."

"Maybe so, Betty Sue." Then his looked at me, "Anyway, the next time you're in town, I would like to hear about it."

I look up at Pa. He responded, "If you want to stay and talk to the sheriff, I guess it's alright. Just be sure to get to the Bouchers before dark and then come on home tomorrow."

"No, no," interrupted the sheriff, "There are feelings still riding pretty high among the young rowdies in town. You'd better drive home together, don't get separated, and be prepared."

The ladies were in the buggies, so we men stepped up and nodding to the sheriff, we started home.

"The next time you're in town, Rob" the sheriff waved and started up the street. Carl pulled out first with his rig, and I turned in behind them, and held up my team so that we would be out of their dust. It also gave us time to enjoy our own little world.

Betty Sue hugged my arm and lay her head on my shoulder, as we rode out into the country. It was not necessary for us to talk to communicate. After a while of just riding along enjoying each other, Betty Sue began to ask pointed questions that would give her an insight into the way I think. "Rob, do you like ranching?"

"A great way of life, don't you agree."

"What do you think of the sheriff's offer to take over his job in a few years?"

"No, I don't mind helping out as a citizen, but that kind of work is not for me. I like the wide open spaces, and a more quiet life."

"I'm glad."

"What's wrong with ranching?"

"Nothing, but it takes a lot of money to start ranching. Most of the ranches around here will only support one family, and your parents are just getting their ranch paid for."

"The Judge ruled that part of Mr. Black's sentence was to cut the rest of the ranch payments in half, for damages to Pa. That will help us get ahead a little. Then I plan to use the bounty money I will collect, to buy some good heifers to go with those I have now. Maybe we can lease some range to the east of us. In a couple years, I'd have enough to start on my own."

"Sometimes my Dad needs a little extra help. I wish you could come over and get better acquainted with him."

Sure, that would be great, only I wouldn't want to charge a friend and neighbor, when he needs help."

"I know, but he wouldn't let you work unless he paid you."

We rode along in silence, while I was thinking. Finally, I broke the silence, "I think I have come up with something, Neither of our ranges are over stocked, If your Dad would let me work for him, when he needs help, in exchange for letting me run a few head on his range, he wouldn't have to use up needed cash, Neither would I need cash to lease range land, and I could buy more cows."

"Oh Rob that is a great idea, I'll talk to Dad about it, May I."

"If you want to."

This early in the morning we didn't need much shade, so Carl just pulled off the road far enough that we wouldn't be disturbed by those going home from town. He pulled up beside a grassy spot and called "Circle the wagons."

Just for fun I drove my buggy in a circle around Carl's when he stopped, then turned them away from the sun.

I jumped down to offer Betty Sue a hand down, when she jumped down from the other side. I watched her for a while as she brought out a blanket for the ground and began to help with the food, Then as I lifted the weight down to the ground to tie the team, I thought now that's the girl I've known all these years. Independent and would run a horse race at the drop of a hat, yet in town she was so dependent, prim and proper.

In the last few years watching her in Church, I never dreamed that she would be interested in being my special girl friend I was still day dreaming, when I heard my mother say, "Rob, breakfast is ready."

I sat down cross legged on one corner of the two blankets that formed a table. After the blessing, Betty Sue served up a plate for me. Then filled her own plate and sat down with her back against mine. "See I have a chair with a back on it."

Her mother looked up with an, "I see."

With the eyes of our parents on us, Pa spoke up, "We are all glad you young people are becoming good friends, but don't go hurrying this friendship too fast."

Betty sue looked back at her mother with a confident 'Don't worry, you know you can trust me,' look. Then she looked right at my mother and blurted out, "Rob is going to buy more cows, with the bounty money he's getting to go with those he has. Then in a couple of years he will have enough to start ranching for himself."

"Pa looked at us and with a frown on his brow and a smile on his lips, asked, "And just where are we going to run all those cows."

"We" Betty Sue started and hesitated to continue, "He could lease some range, or if our fathers agreed, he could run some of them on our range, if there is room and then work for Dad when he needs extra help to pay for it."

"I see you two have it all worked out, but I think Bob and I have to talk this over some first."

Betty Sue knew her father and changed the subject by asking me if I'd like more coffee.

I'm sure this conversation caused our parents to wonder if we were making permanent plans for the two of us, even though we had never admitted even to ourselves that we were. We were always careful to make sure that we never used the plural form when talking of the future.

I guess the breaking of the news that we were thinking ahead and talking it over, must have been of a little concern to both of our parents, for in no time breakfast was over and we were on our way again.

We weren't far down the road when Betty Sue, with both hands in her lap, spoke quietly, "I'm sorry Rob, I guess I should have stayed out of your business and talked to my father when we were alone." Giggling ever so slightly then, with her teasing smile and a shrug of her shoulders. "I think, I scared our parents,"

Again she shrugged, "I think they thought we were planning on setting up housekeeping."

"Well maybe we are, It will take a couple of years to build up a herd and we are only nineteen."

"Why, Robert McCloud, do you always propose on the second date?"

I could feel my face getting red, "Betty Sue, I oh aw, stop your teasing. I've known you for a long time, and I kind of like the idea."

"Maybe we are getting ahead of our selves. When you get to know me, you probably won't even come to see me any more."

"I don't think that will ever happen, the more I see of you the more I want to spend more time with you."

I could tell that she wanted to change the subject, for she was looking around the country side for something to see. "Look at the antelope." She pointed

About twenty-five head looked up and then ran in little circles, then ran around in front of Carl's buggy, the last three darted in front of us, between the two buggies.

"Oh, aren't they beautiful?"

Our horses had been plodding along, since breakfast, now they pricked up their ears, raised their heads and wanted to run, so I let them out a little and caught up with the other buggy.

We pulled along side our parents, and exchanged some light banter, and then having a lighter load, our team pulled out ahead.

We were just far enough ahead when we got to the Boucher's ranch, that we had time for me to water the team while Betty Sue ran to the house to start a light snack. When our parents pulled in, we would have time to rest the horses for an hour or more, and then start home.

Our little family confab at breakfast, must have affected Betty Sue, for she acted as if the date was over, and although she gave me special attention, every thing seemed to have changed. She was acting as if she had forgotten that we has ridden for sometime this morning with her head on my shoulder, It was all strange to me, for the way I was feeling, she would be the only girl for me, and waiting a couple of years would be no problem. I hadn't spent much time with Betty Sue the last few days, but it was still more than I had ever spent with any girl in my life.

After a good snack, Betty Sue and I, moved over to the buggy first. As we walked I asked. "Want to sit with me in Church?"

"Um, if you want to."

"Why shouldn't I?"

She smiled with a shy teasing look, and said, "You won't have your ranch herd large enough to need help for two years."

"Yeah, I know, but I will need all the time I can get to make sure I have the right girl."

"You win, see you Sunday."

Our folks were walking up, so she followed around to watch as I checked the harness and prepared the team for the drive home.

"Rob, I'm sorry I blurted out in front of everyone, our plans for the future."

It wasn't everyone, it was our parents, and we each would have told them anyway. They understand, possibly better that we do,"

"Anyway, I didn't plan it that way."

"No harm done, now we can all plan together."

My folks were already in the buggy, "Well son are you going with us."

I hopped in the back, with my legs over the tail gate, and a wave of my hat.

As a goodbye, Carl called out "Come over next week, Rob, and we'll pick out eight or ten good heifers, that I need to sell."

Betty Sue looked at him in surprise, then with a big smile waved goodbye.

I should have been sleepy on the way home, as tired as I felt. Instead I made myself comfortable and thought of Betty Sue, reliving all the times we were together and everything she did, trying to understand all about her.

On Sunday, I waited around at Church until the Bouchers showed up, then moved away from the guys I was standing with. I stepped over to the rig to help Betty Sue down, and walked her to the Church.

As we walked by the other young people, both groups of boys and Girls quit talking as we passed. Everyone in the Church tried to act normal, but we noticed that the quiet talking became more quiet.

With a pleasant look, Betty Sue, picked a pew, looked to me for approval then sat down. Then looked up again to let me know she was happy. I could tell she was enjoying having everyone notice.

After the service all the ladies greeted us with a polite friendly hand shake. Some of them commented on my busy week.

Chapter 10

The message came out with one of the local ranchers that the sheriff had deposited two thousand dollars in my name at the bank, With this money, I could buy several head of cattle, It wouldn't make me rich, only speed thinks up a little toward the day I could start my own ranch.

On Wednesday, I decided to saddle up and ride over to the Bouchers and look at what he had to sell. When I arrived, Betty Sue helped her mother serve lunch, I was wishing I could see more of her, when she placed a hand on my shoulder and informed me, "Mother and I have a lot to do, so you fellows go make your cattle deal," What a girl! Always being realistic. I have to admit that I was hoping that she would be coming along. She could ride as well as any of us, and I know she had helped her Dad round up before. I knew she was doing the right thing, even though I wanted to be with her as much as possible.

As we walked to the corral, Carl suggested that we ride around to the different herds, pick out stock that we both agreed on, and rope and earmark it on the spot, then we would put my brand on them the next roundup.

"It sounds good to me, the earmark will be fine on the bill of sale."

"By the way Son, we can work out the arrangements on the range lease later on.

We decided that it would be better if I gave my horse a rest and ride one of his ropers.

It took a while to ride out to the first bunch of cows. Carl insisted that he had sold off his cull cows earlier. Since I was starting a herd, he wished to sell me a few of the best looking heifers for a good price.

All afternoon we worked picking out twenty head of the best looking heifers on the range. We rode into the ranch, just as it was getting dark, two tired men and two very tired horses.

When we had washed up and stepped into the kitchen, Betty Sue looked up and asked, "how did it go."

"Fine", I answered.

"I guess it was fine! This young man just bought twenty of the finest head of livestock this side of Kansas City."

From the smile that Mrs. Boucher gave her husband, I could tell that she was in on the plan, and by the way Betty Sue looked from one parent to the other, she had not been told of selling me all young stock, It didn't take a moment for her to understand, though all she said was, "Sit up, I'll serve up the stew."

After the meal was over and Carl had read a chapter for the Bible, Betty Sue and I sat on the porch a while, not having much to say, we walked over to the windmill for a drink that neither of us really wanted. On the way back to the house, she spoke up, "you know what mother and I did today?"

"What?"

"We cleaned up the bunk house and made up a good bed for you. If you are going to be coming over here to work, you will need a place to stay that's comfortable, so maybe you won't get up and leave so early in the morning."

She was a lot like her father, for her excitement had overtones of teasing.

"So you heard what I think about a hammock?"

Our walk led over so she could show me the bunk house. It was clean as any house, with the little room in the back all fixed up like a regular bedroom. In the larger room, where cots lined the wall, there was a little table. On it was a red checkered table cloth and a lamp burning. Someone else had been out walking and had lighted the lamp.

Betty Sue must have seen that I was awkward or something, for she asked, "Want to walk me to the house?"

We walked to the house hand in hand. At the porch she squeezed my hand and said, "Good night".

Back in the bunkhouse, I found the bed comfortable, and in the little time before I fell asleep, I thought if I have to work this hard, I'll never have time for courting.

When day light shining through the window woke me, I felt as rested as if I had slept at home.

At breakfast we discussed what kind of help Carl would need and when he would need it.

"Carl, we see each other almost every Sunday, I can plan my work at home around the work here."

"I don't think it will be too difficult to work out, Most of my work will be breaking colts, and that can be worked in any time."

When breakfast was over, Betty Sue acted as if she had work to do, so she waved goodbye with a, "See, you Sunday."

Carl and I sat at the table with a fresh cup of after breakfast coffee, and I made a 'Pay to the bearer note' for the cattle I had bought, while Carl made out a bill of sale.

"Thank you Rob. In about two weeks I'll have the colts in and we will start breaking those we want to sell." I noticed that he used "we", just like Pa does when he wants to include me in what he is doing.

"I'll plan to come after church on that Sunday, so we can get an early start on Monday morning.

With a half grin, he slapped me on the back and replied, "Well the bunkhouse is all fixed up and ready, so I don't see why not."

I looked for her, but Betty Sue wasn't anywhere around when I saddled up and left, that morning. I remembered her saying, "I'll see you Sunday." That must have been goodbye. I knew she said she was busy, but I couldn't see how she could be that busy. O well, I never could understand girls anyway.

On the way home, I realized that I was well on my way to being a full time rancher. I also remembered how I had wanted to turn down the sheriff, and spend time with Betty Sue. All this would not be happening, if I hadn't given up my personal desires to help someone when asked.

A verse of the Bible came back to me, "Look not every man on his own things, but every man on the things of others."

Right then I was sure glad that my parents had taught me to put others first and let the Lord reward. I never dreamed that it would happen this way.

Until now, I had planned on helping Pa pay for his ranch, then start saving to buy one of my own. With this little help for last weeks work, I would be able to start buying in a couple of years.

Chapter 11

When I got home Pa had the two-year olds, and weaning colts in the corral. He was leaning on the gate watching them when I rode in.

"I thought you might want to pick out some colts for your own work stock. It takes a couple of years to train a good horse, when you can't work them every day."

We watched a while as the colts moved nervously around the corral. There were some very good looking colts in the bunch. I spotted three or four that I wanted to pen up for a closer look.

Just then the dinner bell rang, and we started for the house.

"Have you picked out some you want to keep, for the ranch?" I asked Pa.

"Oh, I think we are set pretty well for this year, so I thought you should take fist pick, then I may save one or two to replace any thing that might go lame on us in the next year or two.

"I think I would like to break a couple of cutting and roping horses this year, and pick out two or three more yearlings to start on next year."

Then he asked, "Do you want your own buggy team?'

"Yeah, I'd like to start breaking them right away."

"I thought you might," we had come to the wash bench and started to washing up.

During lunch we talked over the qualities of the colts, we knew that this was Ma's way of keeping up with what we were doing, and after lunch she would come out to help with the choosing.

"Rob, you go on out and shake out some grain for the colts, so they will take there minds off being penned up. While I help mother with the dishes, then she can come and watch the rodeo.

As I got up from the table I gathered up the plates and silverware and set them beside the dish pan. Mother shooed me out of the way, so I hurried out to the corral, and looked over the colts again, before going to the grain bin for some oats.

I paid close attention to the colts playing, 'boss of the feed bunk'. One of the yearlings had enough spunk that she was not going to let the two year-olds push her out. That one was sure a keeper! I make some mental notes, so that I would remember her later.

Pa had a special attitude about handling colts. He never liked to scare the young ones by roping them the first time they were handled, He had built three corrals each one smaller that the other, so the unbroken horses could be sorted without roping them.

They were still all in the large corral now, so I opened the gate into the next corral, and stood watching a two year old eyeing the gate. When I took a step to the right he darted through. He looked good enough, but I noticed that he didn't have the drive to fight for the oats, so I let him out the side gate into a small pasture where we would hold the stock until they would be gentled down and ridden a few times so someone would buy them and finish training them according to their own taste.

By the time Pa and Ma came out, I had four head turned into the pasture, and most of the rest had finished eating and were milling around.

Pa helped Ma position herself on the top rail of the corral, then sat there with her for a while watching.

I could hear Ma say, "They are better looking this year. There should be several that we could keep to improve our stock, now that Rob's Big Sorrel is old enough to turn out with the herd. I pretended not to hear, for we could have turned him out last spring, but we had decided to wait another year, so he would have the benefit of more training working and roping cattle.

Pa dropped down into the corral and helped her down. The three of us had been sorting stock this way every year since we bought the ranch.

For this job, Ma was dressed like a cowhand, but she only dressed this way when no one was around. One time a few years ago, we were sorting colts when we saw someone riding in. While they were at a distance she disappeared into the house and never came out again. So Pa and I had to finish the job alone.

For several hours I picked out the ones I liked best, and they were moved into the center corral, then opened the gate to the small corral and tried to get only those I wanted into it. That works most of the time with a small group of horses,

Finally I had three two year olds to break for the buggy team. We would pick the best of the three when we started training. With the extra work this summer, I would need at least three of my own horses to train for roping, a heavier work team for heavy loads and mowing hay, and I selected four yearlings to start gentling down for next year. All of these would be branded with my brand so they could be pastured with all the colts we were training.

Pa picked out several head that he wanted to keep, these were turned back into the big corral and the rest were kept in for later breaking to sell.

We decided to wait until tomorrow to do the branding of my stock, so they were left in a corral and fed some hay. The breaking and training would last the rest of the summer. On a horse ranch the horse training never has and end because there are always horses to train. It just becomes a way of life. We were hot and dusty and there were a few other chores to do before dark.

It was dark by the time we had finished our chores. When we came in to clean up, Ma had filled two wash tubs with warm water, and there were clean clothes on the wash bench.

"I think Ma's trying to tell us something, Son and it's not even Saturday night.

"I don't think she wants a couple of smelly old horses in the house."

At supper, Pa and I talked over the work for tomorrow, just as we always did.

"Rob, when we have put your brand on your stock tomorrow, I think we should turn back on the range the ones we want to keep, and spend our time breaking those we want to sell. We can always work in those we want to keep in between other projects."

"I had just taken a mouthful, so I nodded, and when I could, I said, "I'd like to keep in the buggy stock and start them right away, so I have my own team, as soon as possible."

Chapter 12

Now we've all heard stories of breaking horses, by roping and snubbing them to a post, then some great bronco rider gets on and rides them until they stoop bucking. Of course, we are to believe that when the horse knows he can't unseat the rider, and he knows who's boss, and from then on he is broke.

From the time I can remember, I've heard my Grandpa and my Pa say that method is a good way to ruin a good horse and possibly turn him into an outlaw.

I remember a few years ago, when I was leading a colt, that that was already halter broke he reared back and tried to get away, I set my feet and braced the rope over my knee and tried to hold him, I was losing ground, when Grandpa came by and said "let up on the rope, Son." I did and the colt stopped fighting and let me pet him and then he followed without having the rope tight.

Grandpa watched a while, and then said, "If you want a horse to fight back, then just show him you want to fight."

That was a lesson I've never forgotten, although there are times I can just barely remember Grandpa.

I have been helping break horses for several years. So this day was just another day's work that started with breaking colts. I've never gotten over the excitement of the first day of horse breaking. I went around and checked on them, on the way to help Pa milk the three cows that supplied the milk, butter and cheese for out table.

After breakfast, we started a fire just out side the branding chute that we used for horses, and I got out the little c branding iron that I used to brand into the Circle M of Pa's brand to turn it into my Circle Mc brand. The little c fit just inside the circle tight against the leg of the M.

About mid-morning, we were just about done when mother brought out one of the camp coffee pots and set it in the coals of the branding fire to keep it warm, and set a cake pan with a cloth over it on a block near by. Then she waited for us to finish the branding.

Mother often brought out coffee and hot rolls to us when we were working. This was her way of getting out doors and being a part of the work. She had grown up on a farm back in Kentucky and later in Indiana, where she was quite an out of doors girl. She knew horses and could handle them well as any man.

While we were having coffee, a buggy came down the lane. Mother went to the house for more cups. It turned out that it was Mr. and Mrs. Collins from a ranch about ten miles north of us. Word had come to him that Pa might sell his stallion this year, and he would like to see the horse.

Pa and I saddled up a couple of horses for them. He and Collins rode off to bring in the main herd. They were not far away, for they had hung around the corral most of the night, because we had moved over half of the herd into the holding pasture.

While they were gone, I selected the buggy horse that I wanted to start training, then crowded her and the yearlings into box stalls and turned the rest of my horses out into the holding pasture, with the rest of the colts to be broken to ride. Then tying the Big Sorrel with a heavy halter in the small corral; I looked over the old harness in the tack room for something good enough to use to break colts, but wouldn't be a big loss if a colt tore it up.

I had just time to replace a worn strap when I heard the horses coming in, so I opened the gate of the big corral and stood to one side to guide them into the corral.

When the horses were in the corral, I opened the gate to the middle corral about half open, it didn't take but a minute for the Big Sorrel to challenge the range stallion, Before Pa and Collins could dismount and tie up, the range stallion was in the middle corral and the two stallions were trying to get at each other through the high pole corral.

For a minute or two I wasn't sure I was going to get my big sorrel stallion away from the fence and back into his box stall. Once his challenger was removed, the range stallion returned to the side of the corral next to the mares and little colts. He was looking well fed with slick a coat. Collins climbed up where he could see both stallion and his colts. All was quiet for a minute or two, then he looked over at Pa, "How much, will you take for the one the boy put in the barn."

"He belongs to Rob."

I shook my head, "He's a pet, a one man horse."

"Well, McCloud, looks like there is only one choice so, what's he worth?"

"More than most people would pay."

"I can see that."

I could see it was time to find a halter, so I found a good one that we would let go with the stallion, and hung it on a post near by. When I went back into the corral, Collins was counting out some fifty dollar gold pieces into Pa's hand, so I flipped an under handed loop over the stallion's head and led him to heavy post, so he would become accustomed to being tied again so they could lead him home.

"Is he broke to ride too?"

"Yes, I used to work cattle with him up until two years ago, when Rob started breaking his colt. Then I turned him out to keep them apart. That red colt would challenge him before the colt was six months old."

They moved over to the tack room where Pa kept special paper for making out a bill of sale, "I see why you won't sell the colt, I wouldn't either."

Just then, we heard the dinner bell. Ma would never turn a neighbor away without feeding them, whether they bought horses or not.

As we entered the kitchen where we ate, I could see the ladies were having a good visit, while making a big lunch.

During lunch, Collins asked about any cows we wanted to sell, and Pa let him know that we were looking for some to buy also.

Collins shared that he was looking at some over toward Denver, but if they were worth the price he would by them.

"I guess we'll just ask around, there should be a few head for sale."

I left the older folks visiting, while I went out and saddled up Ol' Dan for one more last ride, he and I would have until the colts were ready to sell. I rode out and brought in the colts.

Chapter 13

The next few weeks Pa and I were both very busy working with one colt after another. With both of us working, we could handle every colt every day.

I started my buggy team by harnessing them one at a time with Pa's old gentle team, and driving them around until the younger ones became accustomed to the harness and what was expected of them. Then I worked them one at a time with one of Pa's old gentle ones.

After a few days of that, we hooked them together on a stone boat, with enough weight on it to make it work for them to pull it around. Then one day, I hooked them to an old buckboard that had a spring seat. If the colts ran away and busted it up it would be no great loss,

Things had gone so well the first two weeks that I was making plans to drive my buggy on Sunday. I planned a trial run. Pa and I would drive the few miles to a little store and blacksmith shop that had just opened.

As we started out, things went well until a jack-rabbit jumped up beside the trail and dodged two ways before trying to outrun us. The fillies shied to the left then broke into a run. I fought them for a quarter of a mile before they settled down. They were in a nervous lather when we pulled up in front of the new store.

Just then Mr. D. who lived across the road, stepped out of the store, and greeted us with his high squeaky voice. The fillies shied back toward the road just as Pa stepped down from the buggy. At Mr. D's "Hold 'm, boy", they bolted.

Every time I tried to hold them back, the one on the right would rear right up and walk on her hind legs. So I just turned them loose and let them run, hoping I would be able to keep them on the road. When they slowed to a trot, I swung them into a wide circle and headed them back to the store. When we came to the store they were doing fine. Mr. D. was no where in sight and Pa was standing in the door waiting. The one on the right was still spooky of the strange surroundings. The more I tried to pull her up to the store, the more she fought back, so I circled out for another try. After two tries I ended up with one horse and one wheel on the boardwalk. Before she had time to spook again, Pa stepped into the buckboard and said "Take 'em home."

We were off again and by the time we arrived home, the team had settled down and were behaving like they should, but I must say, that I was disappointed. I knew by now that I would be riding instead of driving, come Sunday.

I also knew that I would be trying out the other filly to match the one on the left. I sure didn't want a spooky one for a driving team. Pa helped me rub down team and turn them out, and then left to take the few groceries to the house.

I saddled up one of the two year olds that we had been working with to sell, and rode around the corral a few times, then opened the gate and headed up the trail to see how he would do. He hadn't learned much of what the reins were for and when I tried to get him to run, he did his best to unseat me, but the ride to the Bouchers did him a lot of good.

My work with Carl was much the same as at home, getting the colts ready to drive and ride. The days were so long that about the only time I had left to see Betty Sue was at meal time and on Sundays. When night came I was too tired to sit up and visit.

In a few weeks, Pa decided that it was time to take a few head to the livery stable to see what we could get for them. What they would bring would depend on how well they were trained, for there were plenty of horses in the country, Not many of them that were for sale were trained well enough to be ready for cutting and roping.

Pa had decided to sell one of the older work teams that were so well trained that they would stand for hours hitched to a wagon with the lines tied to the standard. He also was selling a couple of the mares that were good ropers, but were also brood stock. By selling old stock, we could get horses to town before those who were breaking young stock for sale.

We left early on Monday morning with four horses tied behind the wagon that Pa had gotten from a neighbor in a horse trade. I decided to ride one of the colts and lead another two. If they didn't sell we could ride them home. By that time they would be ready to start training for roping. If everything went well we would be home late that evening and I would stay over at Carl's for another day or two.

Our stop at Carl's was short. Betty Sue came out to look at the horses, and we chatted for a while.

Carl said, "I'll be ready next week, to do the same thing."

"Let Rob help. It is always better to have someone along when moving horses, just in case you have trouble." Pa replied as he started the wagon down the lane with his unusual cargo.

If we sell them, I'll come back here to help with your colts."

"We'll see. If you could help a few more days, they might be ready sooner."

I gathered up the lead ropes of the two horses I was leading, then returned Betty's wave, and swung unto the saddle of the colt that I was breaking. He decided that he was not interested in letting me lead the other two. He began to kick and we took after Pa at a pace that would catch him before he reached the main road.

Our first stop was at the livery stable where we left the rig and all of our stock, except the two sea-soned ropers. These we saddle up and rode over to the restaurant, where we tied them to the hitching rail, entered and ordered lunch.

Jake Yoder from over east of out ranch, came in and sat at our table. We began talking abut horses, Pa asked how many horses he was selling, Jake said he was selling, but he could sure us a better roping horse. He had lost one of his best ones to a broken leg.

"You should look over those tied out front."

"You're not selling you seasoned ropers?" he frowned, "What's wrong with them?"

"They are good mares, but not our best. Rob is breaking several young ones for us this year."

"I'll take a look at them when we've finished this coffee." He looked out the window, "Have they been running with your range Stallion?"

"When ever we're not using them."

Jake look out at them again, "that makes it more interesting."

Pa laughed, "Just so you don't go into competition with my good strain of horses."

Jake change the subject, "Dan Webb is looking for something to train for rodeo calf roping, that he can train for his type of roping."

"Rob has been riding one that fits that description."

After lunch, Jake looked over the horses outside, then after looking at their teeth he mounted his choice and turned it on its back legs and broke into a run down the street. On the way back he shook out the rope I had on the saddle and dropped a loop over my head. The horse stopped and backed into the rope so fast that it made Jake grunt.

As he swung down, he turned to Pa, "don't think I need to ride the other one, this one is sound and I like the looks of her."

"Yes she's sound and a good worker too."

"I'll take that one, but I'm afraid I can't pay you until I sell some colts."

I decided to enter into the deal, "How many two year olds would you trade for this one?"

"Do you think you can handle any more, with those you are breaking for Carl?"

"I believe I can, they will bring more, when they are well broke, and that will buy more calves."

"You want more calves; I've got some I'll trade if you throw in the other one."

Pa turned, "I'll go see what kind of deal I can make with Joe down at the livery."

When Jake and I finished our deal, I had make arrangements to deliver the ropers when we came to pick up the heifers I had traded for.

I left Jake and crossed to the sheriff's office to see if he was in.

"Hi there Rob! You come in to trade jobs with me?"

"No, we are selling horses."

"That Big Sorrel, would suit me fine. What'd you want for him?"

"Sorry, Pa sold his range stallion, so the sorrel will take over his job on the range."

He turned to the coffee pot, want a cup?"

I picked up a cup that looked clean, and he filled it.

The sheriff sat down in his big wooden swivel chair, "You know Rob, my mother had the kind of faith that you have, but I sort of followed my father, who never cared much for God, until just before he died. Somehow it wasn't that important to me, until I saw what it had done for you.

"If your mother was a Christian, she probably told you that Jesus came to die that we could be forgiven."

"Yeah, when I was a boy I remember learning a verse about God loving the world, but I guess I never thought that included me."

I finished the verse, "That He gave His only begotten son that whosoever believeth in Him has everlasting life."

"Yeah, that's the one; I used to know that one. I believe there is a God, and I've been good as I can be. Well I was a little wild when I was young, I've really not done anything real bad, and if I wasn't a law abiding citizen, they sure wouldn't make me sheriff."

"I'm sure God appreciates your being good, but the verse say's "That whosoever believeth in Him shall not perish."

"Yeah, I see that. I believe in Jesus. He was a good man and great teacher, although I don't understand most of his teaching."

Just then a deputy came in and helped himself to the coffee.

"Watch the store Jim; I want to have a talk with Rob."

We went out the side door, and down the alley in the direction of the livery stable.

We hadn't gone far when the sheriff asked, "There must be more to it, or I don't have enough faith or something."

"In Ephesians two, verses eight through ten." I answered, "The Bible says 'For by grace are you saved by faith, that not of your self, it is the gift of God. Not of work lest any man should boast. For we are his workmanship, created in Christ Jesus unto good work, which God had foreordained that we should walk in them."

"I've tried but I just don't have that kind of faith."

"But you see faith is a gift,

"But how do I get the gift of faith?"

I pushed back my hat the band was getting hot and sweaty, "Faith is being united with Christ", Oh, I thought, 'how can I ever explain this so that he will under stand."

You see, Sheriff, "when we invite the Lord Jesus into our lives, He gives us the gift of being united with Him. This is Faith, when we come to the Lord he gives us the privilege of sharing in the benefits of His death for our sin and His resurrection, so that we also are given new life in Him. When this happens, I Corinthians 5:17 says, "We become new creatures, old things pass away and everything becomes new."

"You remember the verse you quoted about God loving the World?

"Yeah."

"It also says that whosoever believeth in Him hath everlasting life. You said you believed in God. Do you under stand that if you really believe in Jesus Christ you would invite him into your life to give you the gift of his work for you, by dying in your place that you can have a new life that is the everlasting life.

"Oh, that is the difference?"

"When you understand God, you understand that when His spirit is united with your spirit, that makes you see everything different and He begins to change our attitude and thinking to make you more like Himself. He leaves you in full control but gives you the power to do something that you have never been able to do before. That is to live the way God wants you to live.

Why don't you just ask Him to come into your life?

"Now that makes sense."

We were walking down the alley, and he just kept on walking, as he began to pray, "God, this young man has just made more sense than anyone ever has. This old reprobate needs a lot of forgiving, and I would like to have you come in and give me the faith that this guy has, for it reminds me of my own mother's faith. Thank you for answering her prayers. I want you to come into my life and give me your gift of life."

He reach over and slapped me on the back, "Rob my boy, I just knew by the way you acted that there was something more to your life. I must admit that I wanted that kind of confidence in my life."

"Thank you", I didn't know what else to say, "That kind of confidence comes from faith in Christ."

"I know that now. Thanks to you."

The sheriff, thought for a while then broke the silence with, "Ya know son, I think I'll get out my mother's old Bible and see why she read it so much."

"That's a good start."

We had come to the livery stable by then, and Pa and Joe met us at the door of the barn.

The sheriff, walked right up to Pa and shook his hand and said, "That son of yours just did me one of the biggest favors of my life."

Pa not wanting to embarrass him replied, "I guess that means you received the gift he had to offer."

"Sure did, and I can tell you, If God can love this old reprobate enough to change his life, I'll sure never be sorry."

Joe, the livery man, stepped over and offered his hand to the sheriff, "I'm glad to see you come to Christ. Some of us have been praying for you for some time, but it just never seems the right time to talk about it."

"Well I never! You mean you, too?" If that, don't beat all!"

"Come on Sheriff, we will walk you back to the office, our horses are tied up there at the hitching rail."

"On the way back to the sheriff's office Pa told us, "I have sold the team and wagon for a good price to Joe, we'll leave the rest of them with him. I told him what I wanted for them and he will get the best price possible."

"I guess we can ride home the ones I sold to Jake. I told him we would deliver them when we pick up the heifers I traded for."

"So, he took both, did he? Did you get a good trade?"

"I think so."

The sheriff just looked on, "You got a good rancher there McCloud. I believe he is too good a man to be sheriff any way."

I could tell the sheriff was back to his old joking about me in front of my Pa, and knew that it was his way of bragging on me, without sounding like it."

At the sheriff's office, he shook our hands and thanked us again. We told him goodbye and stopped over at the general store to pick up a few thing that Ma needed, and headed home.

By the time we reached Carl's he had decided to wait and see how our horses sold. Then he asked if I would help train his colts for cutting and roping, then they should bring more.

I decided to stay a few days and give Carl's colts a work out. So Pa took our horses home. He knew that for the rest of the summer there would be colts that would need to be ridden out, and a good way to do that was to ride then several miles home.

Chapter 14

For the rest of the summer, Betty Sue and I found time for a occasional picnic on a Sunday afternoon. I was able to plan the work days for Carl so that I could take her home after Church on Sunday, then work with Carl a day or two before returning home to get my own work done.

Twice during the summer, she came home with me and helped my mother a day or two.

Then one day I had been out on the range working the kinks out of one of the stubborn colts. It had taken most of the afternoon and I returned about supper time. There was a strange horse tied to the windmill, and a stranger about my age was sitting on the porch talking to Betty Sue.

It's hard to tell how I felt, but I had a strange feeling, like I'd been kicked in the stomach, and one thing I was sure of. I didn't like someone else thinking he could come courting Betty Sue.

I worked the colt around the corral a few time, trying to decide what to do. Carl was in the barn finishing up the chores. Finally, I decided to lead the colt out to the windmill for a sip of water. While I was there I could check the brand on the visitor's horse, It was the lazy T, a ranch over west. I had heard that they had a son about my age, but I didn't know him. He had not gone to our school, and right now I didn't want to know him.

I put the colt away, filled a pail at the windmill and headed for the bunk house to wash up and change clothes before I went in. These long days of work get a man sort of dirty and sweaty.

When I got to the house, Betty Sue was gone and Carl was talking to the stranger.

"Rob, this is Bill, our neighbor to the west."

We shook hands, I said nothing.

"Rob has some cows here on the ranch. He was out checking them out."

"When we were called for supper, Bill got up and joined us. I didn't like it, even knowing that it was the custom of the range to feed travelers at meal time.

Betty Sue smiled when we came in, but one look at me and she all of sudden sobered up, then acted like she never knew me. I watched Bill and noticed that he never took his eyes off Betty Sue.

I didn't have anything to say all during supper, Carl tried to keep the conversation going but no one seemed to be interested in what he was saying and I wasn't hungry.

After supper when Carl read from the Bible I noticed that Bill wasn't listening, just sitting there watching Betty Sue.

As soon as supper was over, I got up an went out to the porch, Carl and Bill followed.

Bill spoke first, "came over to see if you had any colts to break, we are pretty much caught up at home."

"No, I guess not. We've got it under control, Rob is helping out. Most of the hard work if done already, with just the training left."

Bill stepped to the screen door and said, "Good by Betty Sue. I'll ride over again sometime."

When he was mounted up and was riding down the lane, Carl chuckled, "I think he's trying to beat your time."

It wasn't funny. Without a word, I stood up and started to leave. The screen door opened and Betty Sue stopped me with a very concerned voice, "Rob".

Carl excused himself, and Betty Sue and I sat on the new porch swing that Carl had just built.

After a long while, Betty Sue broke the silence, What is the matter Rob?"

"I just don't like him hanging around."

"We went to grade school together. I haven't seen him for two or three years."

"Just the same, I don't like the way he was always looking at you."

"Rob, I believe you're jealous."

I felt like something had hit me in the stomach. I didn't like the way I felt. I was hurt, confused, like I had been betrayed. I stood up and my voice sounded more sharp than I intended, "I guess you'll have to decide who you want," As soon as I said it, I wished I hadn't for she answered me in kind, "you don't own me Rob McCloud."

I couldn't believe what was happening, I'd had the wind knocked out of me before, but it didn't hurt as much as this. I couldn't believe this. I stood up and walked straight for the barn.

"Rob?"

I wanted to stop, but I kept walking. I heard the screen door.

My eye were blinded with tears, as I saddled a colt that needed a work out and lead him to water and headed for home on the run.

The more I rode the more I couldn't believe it had happened. I knew I was in love with Betty Sue, and I thought she was in love with me. Then I wondered what made her change he mind. Girls! I never could understand them, anyway. Just when you thought you knew them, they changed without warning.

Long before I got home, both my horse and I were exhausted. I quit trying to think and would have gone to sleep in the saddle, but the colt had never been here before and didn't know the way. Just as I was about to doze off, the colts head came up and his nostrils flared then he laid back his ears, jerked his head down, humped his back and tried to unseat me. When that didn't work he would stop still and refuse to move, then started to lay down. I jumped off and he sprang to his feet, with me back in the saddle.

I was awake now, for I knew this horse was a smart one, and would need my full attention the rest of the way home.

On the second day, Mother asked me when we were alone, "Has something happened with Betty Sue and you?"

I always told her everything, so I told her what had happened.

"Oh Rob, did you stop to think how it must have hurt her for you to even think that she would be interested in someone else?"

"No, I guess I couldn't think straight."

"You two have talked about being in love, haven't you?"

"No".

"Have you told her that you love her and asked her to wait for you?" You know, a lot of her friends have gotten married at her age."

"But she knows how I feel."

"yes, I think so, but can she be sure, if you never tell her?"

"She has no business letting Bill come and see her, she might change her mind about me."

"Do you really believe that?"

"I don't know."

"Then you had better make up your mind, what you believe."

"Whose side you on, anyway?"

"Don't you know?"

"Oh I don't know anything any more! I don't think I'll ever understand women."

"Rob, it isn't like you to fuss over things, instead of praying about them,"

"I know." I stood up and headed toward the barn, and more hard work. On the way, I turned all my worries over to God.

On Sunday, I hitched up my buggy, with my new team, and tied the colt of Carl's on behind.

Pa came out of the house, "I don't intend to tell you how to run your business, but if I were you, I wouldn't want that colt along to cause problems. I don't think it's good idea to have a young lady along when you're trying to handle three green horses."

I stood a while and pondered what he said, then untied the colt. Turned him back in the pasture and prepared for Church.

Betty Sue was standing on the Church steps, when I tied up to the rail. When I came around the corner, she had gone inside, and the girls that stayed out side all smiled and said, "Hi, Rob."

Stepping inside, I saw that Betty Sue had found a place by her folks, Carl nodded recognition, When I sat by Betty Sue, she stiffened, did not look at me, and just stared straight ahead.

I leaned over toward her and whispered, "I'm sorry." She ignored me.

When the service was over, we stood and filed out, she followed her parents out, as if I wasn't there.

Carl always stood around and talked after Church, but I think he knew I needed to talk to Betty Sue, so he led his family straight to the buggy.

When we were away from the crowd I faced Betty Sue, "May I drive you home?"

"You don't need to, I can ride with my parents. Besides I believe you have a horse that belongs to us. You can just ride him home, pick up your cows, and get them off our range."

"All right young lady, that's far enough," Carl interrupted.

She turned her back, and took one step toward their buggy.

"Betty Sue," my voice, didn't sound like me. It was more like Pa's voice when he was about to object to something I wanted to do. I wasn't going to give in.

"I'd like to drive you home so I could tell you how sorry I am, for my actions the last time.

Her mother gave her a little shove in the direction of my buggy, "Go ahead, your father and I want to greet our friends. We'll be along in a little while."

She walked stiffly ahead of me to my buggy, I helped her up and handed her the reins and said, "Hold them up so they don't leave without me." Very carefully, I untied the team and with deliberation, tied the hitching rope to the harness, backed the team slowly away from the hitching rail, so as to not excite them.

Just as I stepped up and turned to sit down, she slapped the colts with the reins and shouted, "get up."

I sat down with a bang hard enough to break something, and grabbed the reins. By this time we were turning on two wheels toward our place. Betty Sue was hanging onto the seat with one hand and onto me with the other. We swung a wide circle, headed toward her place, passing rigs in the first quarter of a mile from the Church, then pulled up behind Sam and Alice, who had just started going together, Sam's old buggy didn't have a top, so we could see him coax his team into a run to stay ahead of us. When he did, Alice turned and grabbed him around the shoulders and buried her head at the back of his neck.

My team were still trying to run away, so I let them out and in no time we were running neck and neck. After a short run, Sam pulled his seasoned team up and my colts slowed down too. We all had a good laugh.

Betty Sue, who was enjoying the whole thing, turned to Alice and teased, "Why Alice, I didn't know!"

Alice composed her posture, but her face was now a bright red, Sam only grinned at me and said, "Want to do that again?"

To this, Alice answered, "NO."

"Sam winked, then nodded and we pulled away from them, knowing without looking that they had turned off in the direction of Alice's place. Sam and I had been good friends for a long time.

We were alone now and the colts had quieted down some, so I turned to Betty Sue, to apologize, "I hadn't meant to hurt you."

"What kind of a girl do you think I am?"

"I've always thought you were too good and to beautiful for a guy like me, and just a little afraid someone would come along that you would like better."

"Do you think that I would like that tobacco chewing, dirty cowboy, better than you?"

"No, that's just it I didn't think. You see, I don't know girls very well. Until now, I just watched them from a distance, and I don't have any sisters, My little sister died when we were small on our way here from back east. All I know, is that when I saw you with that guy, I felt like I had been kicked in the stomach by an angry mule."

"Oh, Rob, I'm sorry, I thought you knew how I felt about you. I was so angry that you would think I could be interested in anyone else. I was just being polite to him."

"I don't think he knew that, and any way. The polite thing to do with a guy like that would be to send him packing."

"Ma had given him coffee, and he just didn't get up and leave."

"He didn't know about us and I'm sure he wouldn't care if he did. He didn't strike me as that kind."

Betty Sue, took my arm above the elbow like she always had lain her head on my shoulder. I never kissed her before, so leaning over I gave her a peck on the forehead She looked up and I was just ready to try for her lips when the buggy wheel hit something and the colts jumped. I had to pay attention to my driving. Soon we pulled off the main road to our favorite picnic place, I swung the colts around to a stop an stepped out of the buggy and helped Betty Sue down. She looked at the back of the buggy, "Oh, did you bring a lunch?"

"No."

I didn't want to take any chances, so I wrapped my wrist around the lines, then placed them between my fingers, reaching out with my other arm, drew her to me, and planted a kiss on her lips. For a second she froze, then retuned my kiss with passion.

Now about this time, I was wishing I had traded teams with Pa and had his old gentle team, so I could forget the team and tend to the things at hand. Maybe it was a good thing, for that last kiss had left me a little light headed, In fact, I stayed that way all the rest of the day.

I don't even remember how we got back in the buggy, or what we said on the way home. I vaguely remember that Betty Sue never let go of my arm and most of the way her head was on my shoulder. I tried a couple of times to drive with one hand, but the colts wouldn't let me.

I came back to earth again as we pulled around the curve into the lane, and saw a horse tied to the windmill and knew who was waiting on the porch swing, although we were too far away to see him.

I turned to Betty Sue, " I love you very much, will you wait a couple of years to marry me so I can get a house built and a ranch started.?"

"Oh Rob I love you, let build the house together."

When she looked up at me, I didn't care if the colts did run away, I confirmed our agreement with a kiss. In response, she put both arms around my neck and we enjoyed the best kiss yet.

We pulled the team in beside Bill's horse at he hitching rail, and together tied them up. The Bouchers were coming up the lane as we came up to the porch.

Betty Sue greeted Bill with a, "Hi Bill, you are the first to know, Rob and I just got engaged."

"W e l l g o o d f o r y o u," he said with disgust and made straight for his horse and rode toward home.

I watched him ride off and remarked, "He must be having a bad day or something."

Betty Sue, gave a little giggle and squeezed my hand. We were still holding hands when her folks came up to the house.

"I guess he's not staying for dinner," smiled Carl at his own joke.

"No", added Betty Sue, We just walked up and told him about our engagement and he just got up and left.

"Your, What?" her mother looked at her with surprise, "I thought you were mad at each other."

Betty Sue made a face that looked a little like a smirk and a frown.

"So! When is this big day, that I'm supposed to give permission for?"

"Oh Daddy, we have to build a house first, and get a ranch started,"

"Well then. If that's the case, maybe we can all work together."

Carl shook my hand while he drew Betty Sue to him and Mrs. Boucher gave me a motherly hug. Then Carl spoke. Well now, lets thank the Lord, together."

We all stood with arms around each other while Carl thanked the Lord for the way He worked in the lives of all that put their trust in Him.

When the prayer was over Betty Sue looked up into my face, "Oh Rob, in a couple of days we could take the buggy back. Let's saddle up and ride over to your place in the morning. I think I know how your mother feels about us, I can't wait to share the news with your folks, and have their blessing,"

CPSIA information can be obtained at www.ICGtesting.com
Printed in the USA
BVOW021456240712

296068BV00001B/2/P